TEN KINGS

And the Worlds They Ruled

ALSO BY MILTON MELTZER

Carl Sandburg: A Biography

Case Closed: The Real Scoop on Detective Work

Dorothea Lange: A Photographer's Life

Driven from the Land: The Story of the Dust Bowl

Frederick Douglass in His Own Words

Langston Hughes: A Biography

Lincoln in His Own Words

The Many Lives of Andrew Carnegie

Piracy and Plunder: A Murderous Business

Slavery: A World History

Ten Queens: Portraits of Women of Power

There Comes a Time: The Struggle for Civil Rights

They Came in Chains: The Story of the Slave Ships

A Thoreau Profile (with Walter Harding)

Weapons and Warfare: From the Stone Age to the Space Age

Witches and Witch-hunts: A History of Persecution

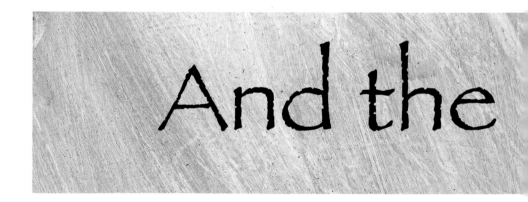

ORCHARD BOOKS • NEW YORK

An Imprint of Scholastic Inc.

by MILTON MELTZER

TEN KINGS
Worlds They Ruled

illustrated by
Bethanne Andersen

Library of Congress Cataloging-in-Publication Data
Meltzer, Milton, date.
Ten kings: and the worlds they ruled / Milton Meltzer; illustrated by Bethanne Andersen.—lst ed.   p.   cm.
Includes bibliographical references and index.
Contents: Introduction—Hammurabi—David—Alexander the Great—Attila—Charlemagne—Kublai Khan—
Mansa Musa—Atahualpa—Louis XIV—Peter the Great.
ISBN 0-439-31293-0 (alk. paper)
1. Kings and rulers—Biography—Juvenile literature. [1. Kings, queens, rulers, etc.] I. Title: 10 kings. II. Andersen,
Bethanne, date, ill. III. Title.
D107.M45   2002   920.02—DC21   2001-033202

10 9 8 7 6 5 4 3 2 1   02 03 04 05

Printed in Singapore   46
First edition, April 2002

Book design by Mina Greenstein. The text of this book is set in 13 point Bembo.
The illustrations are oil paintings done on gesso.

In memory of one of the greatest kings—
Martin Luther King, Jr.
—M.M.

To good men who teach their sons
to walk with compassion
—B.A.

CONTENTS

Introduction

THIS BOOK IS ABOUT POWER—POWER IN THE HANDS OF KINGS.

The king, in the times covered in this book, was the supreme ruler over a nation or a territory. His rank was higher than that of any other secular authority—prince, baron, duke, lord. Kings have ruled in almost every part of the world. Usually the kingship was hereditary: the king's power was passed on to his first-born son.

Kingship often had a religious significance: the king was seen as the mediator between his people and their god, or as the god's representative on Earth. In ancient Egypt the pharaoh himself was looked upon as divine. He was god on Earth. That idea of a divine ruler on Earth carried over into ancient Greece as well and was later revived by some of the Roman emperors. When kings came to the throne in medieval Europe, they were anointed at their coronation, a ceremony meant to give divine authority to their rule.

How did kingship arise? Long, long ago most people lived in small bands, roving about to gather food wherever they could, while some hunted or fished. Farming was invented about twelve thousand years ago. As people learned to domesticate plants and animals, they settled into permanent communities. And as some of these villages grew larger and larger, they became cities.

In smaller societies, men of superior strength or achievements rose to the top. We generally refer to such leaders as chieftains. When societies became larger and more complex, kingdoms developed. Kings made the rules by which their people lived, and carried on wars to protect their realms or expand their power.

Kings have usually been considered special and unique. They were supposed to be different from and superior to ordinary people. In all kingdoms loyalty to the king was the supreme political value. His was the power, and no one had better question it. People showed their respect for his authority in such ways as bowing before him, kneeling before him, or kissing his hand, while constantly declaring loyalty and devotion.

Many nations still have kings. Even though a king may not directly handle governmental or administrative duties, he stands above everyone else as the symbol of national identity and an expression of the people's political unity.

This book tells the story of ten kings, who were shaped by the worlds into which they were born and who, in turn, reshaped those worlds to a degree. As you'll see, kings, like the rest of us, are complex human beings: good, bad, a mixture of the two; benevolent, cruel, brilliant, stupid. Each monarch's story may help you grasp how political leaders use and abuse power. Remote as the times in this book may seem, the stories featured here all have elements that may illuminate what goes on in our own democratic society, where an elected president, not a king, is the head of state.

The index will be useful to readers who may want to compare various aspects of the kings' lives. For those wishing to learn more about a king, the note on sources and the bibliography should be helpful.

Because historians are sometimes uncertain about the dates of a king's lifespan—especially for those monarchs who lived in ancient times—the dates of each king's reign are given at the beginning of each chapter.

TEN KINGS

And the Worlds They Ruled

Hammurabi

Reigned 1792–1750 B.C.

The first city-states in history, ruled by kings, developed in Mesopotamia. The best known of those kings was Hammurabi. The code of laws he established is famous as one of the world's oldest.

Mesopotamia is a region in the Middle East. It has been known by many names: Chaldea, Akkad, Sumer, Babylonia, Assyria. Today it is called Iraq. It consists of a patchy floodplain with wide-open frontiers on two of its sides. On the south is desert, and looming over the east is a plateau. Two great rivers, almost parallel, run the length of the land. They are the Tigris and the Euphrates, which flow together into the Persian Gulf.

Babylon was the capital of Hammurabi's kingdom. Its hanging gardens were one of the wonders of the ancient world. Today little remains of the city's legendary glory—desert sand has swallowed up much of it.

How did the civilization of Babylonia develop? Around thirteen thousand years ago wandering tribes, whose hunting, fishing, and farming had assured a reliable supply of food, began to live in settlements. The tribes were made up of clans or kinship groups, small enough so that everyone knew everyone else. At the head of the tribe was the "big man." He held no formal office. He was

1

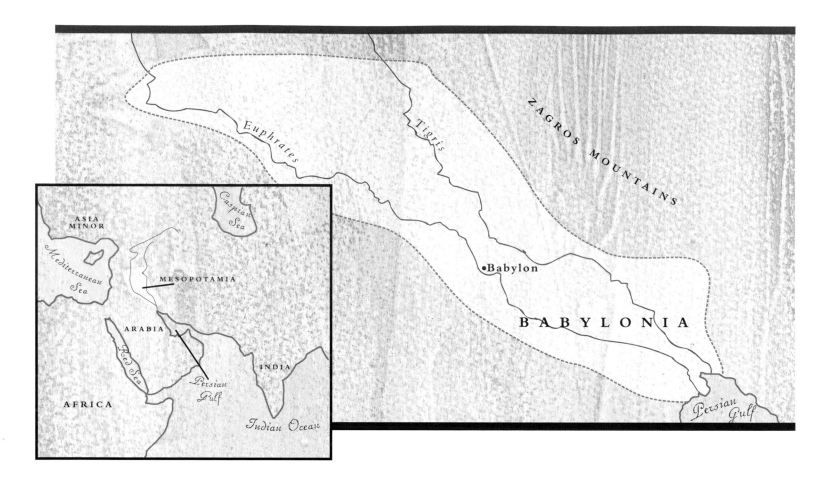

not elected nor did he inherit the position. Gradually, around seventy-five hundred years ago, tribes grew into chiefdoms. Their leaders had a role in collecting and redistributing food and goods. "With the rise of chiefdoms," says the scientist Jared Diamond, "people had to learn, for the first time in history, how to encounter strangers regularly without attempting to kill them."

The chief had a monopoly on the use of force. He held his job by hereditary right. He was the recognized authority who made all the major decisions. He had a title equivalent to *king*.

With the advance of technical skills the villagers were able to smelt iron, work copper, and manufacture textiles and pottery. Many moved from small villages into large cities. Monumental buildings, chiefly temples, were built of kiln-fired bricks. Silver, lead, gold, and lapis lazuli came into common use. Giant steps forward were the inventions of a solar calendar and pictographic writing on clay tablets.

Over the centuries the kings of Mesopotamia would consolidate these city-states into new kingdoms centered on splendid capitals. Babylon came to dominate the region's southern half. It had once been an unimportant town about fifty miles south of present-day Baghdad. Hammurabi was the sixth in line in a dynasty of rulers founded in 1850 B.C. There is little to say about his childhood or youth because no records of it have been found.

When he came to the throne in 1792 B.C. his state was ringed by aggressive rival powers. He destroyed them one by one. He united the several ethnic groups of Mesopotamia under a single government. He made social and administrative reforms that concentrated power in the king's hands and still gave play to local custom and management.

Hammurabi understood that conquest did not bring peace or contentment unless it was followed by the creation of a just political system. A good king must take practical measures to secure the domestic, industrial, and commercial welfare of the people as a whole. Hammurabi developed the natural resources of every district, extending irrigation so that agriculture would prosper and goods could move quickly and easily along a system of canals. He was a kind of benevolent despot, a patriarch in complete control of his national family.

At the end of his forty-two-year reign Hammurabi had expanded Babylonia from a territory less than fifty miles in radius to a realm stretching from the Persian Gulf to the borders of modern Turkey. The empire was about seven hundred miles long and one hundred miles wide, the largest state to appear up to that time. A brilliant diplomat, Hammurabi knew when to give and bend, and when to attack. He made political and military alliances, but would break them whenever it helped his drive to power.

How do we know all this? It comes from the findings of archaeologists. Digs in the region have uncovered not only roads, houses, palaces, temples, statues, and stelae (carved commemorative slabs), but also imperial archives of tens of thousands of clay tablets.

The tablets were inscribed with pictographs, the forerunners of cuneiform script. The earliest were basically pictures of objects, often with symbols representing numbers. These were administrative records of grain, cattle, and other goods. Later pictographs came to stand not only for the object pictured but also for certain sounds. When pictograph writing developed into cuneiform, the world had its first written language, an immensely important leap forward in civilization. The invention of writing was one of humankind's greatest achievements. It made it possible to preserve thoughts and experiences and to pass on hard-earned wisdom to future generations.

As cuneiform writing became vital to the kingdom, an increasingly important profession was that of scribe, which required intense training. Aspiring scribes attended school from childhood to young manhood. They went to class year-round, with only six days off per month—three holy days and three free days. Learning language was the primary course, but students also learned about geography, mathematics, law, medicine, and astronomy.

The training was monotonous and the discipline harsh. Pupils were caned for talking without permission or for hanging around in the street. But if they made it through to graduation, they became highly respected and well-paid professionals, experts who could run estates, mediate disputes, survey fields, and settle claims.

The Babylonian clay tablets unearthed by archaeologists include hundreds of official letters that date from Hammurabi's reign. Many are directives to officials in the conquered provinces. These letters show that the king was not only a powerful warrior but also a hardworking manager who cared for the welfare of his people. He gave as much attention to minor personal matters of his subjects as he did to tax collecting and the upkeep of his country's vital irrigation systems.

There were three distinct classes in Hammurabi's kingdom. At the top: the aristocrats, the rich and powerful families. From among them, the king selected his temple priests, counselors, ambassadors, generals, and administrators. Their wealth came from large landholdings. At the bottom: the slaves. Like every other ancient civilization and many of modern times, Babylonia rested on slavery. Slaves were the property of the palace, the temple, or the wealthy establishment. The average household too had slaves. Some slaves had been prisoners of war; others, free citizens who had sold themselves, their children, or the whole family into slavery. The lives of Babylonian slaves do not seem to have been as harsh as those of slaves in the Americas. The master's ownership of his slaves was not absolute. While the law encouraged slavery, it recognized that slaves were valuable to society and needed protection. Slaves could legally engage in business, borrow money, and purchase their freedom. They had legal rights, though narrow ones.

Between the two extremes was the mass of the common people: workers, farmers, cattle breeders, fishers, carpenters, smiths, potters, brick makers, scribes, architects. Many who had specialized skills were employed by landlords, temples, or merchants. Craftspeople had their own shops or sold their wares in bazaars.

Two occupations were crucial to the kingdom's success. Farmers raised the grains and other crops that put food on the tables of everyone from king to commoner to slave. Merchants traveled far and wide, at home and abroad, exchanging the country's surplus goods for products that could not be obtained locally, such as the metal, stone, and timber needed to maintain an army and build temples to the gods. Behind every merchant were many artisans needed to produce exportable goods and to work up the imported raw materials.

Ordinary working people lived in plain single-story houses of mud brick. The better-off had two-story homes of kiln-baked, sun-dried brick, whitewashed inside and out. The interiors of these houses were protected from the intense heat of the region by walls sometimes six feet thick. Kings of course lived in luxurious style. One palace unearthed by archaeologists was a huge complex covering almost seven acres. It had nearly three hundred rooms and open courtyards. The rooms were beautifully decorated with wall paintings.

Justice in Babylonia was based on a system of common law handed down over the years and modified to meet changing social and economic conditions. Every ruler applied the laws of the kings before him, made adjustments in them, and added new rulings for situations without precedent. Near the end of his reign Hammurabi created his law code by assembling rules that were already current; he did not originate them. He had the code carved on stelae and placed them in temple courtyards for the public to consult. He meant to show that he had given his people justice as the gods willed it.

temple courtyard

One of these stelae, seven feet three inches high and conical in shape, was found by French archaeologists in 1901 and placed in the Louvre Museum in Paris. At the top is carved a bas-relief showing Hammurabi in prayerful attitude toward what is either the sun god or the god of justice, seated on a throne. Below, the stela is inscribed all around with vertical columns of text, some four thousand lines of it.

In a prologue Hammurabi boasts that Babylon is now "supreme in the world." The prologue goes on to say that the gods instructed Hammurabi "to make justice appear in the land, to destroy the evil and the wicked that the strong might not oppress the weak, to rise like a sun god . . . to give light to the land."

Hammurabi's code consists of almost three hundred articles dealing with all aspects of everyday life in Babylonia—wages, divorces, fees for medical care, and many other matters. The code describes all kinds of crimes and misdemeanors and specifies the punishment for each. Clearly Mesopotamian society had its full quota of murderers, thieves, con artists, and adulterers, and a range of corruption all too familiar in our own time.

Punishment was diverse and harsh, with mutilation or death often called for. In essence, the code demands an eye for an eye and a tooth for a tooth. (Five centuries later, the biblical code of Exodus echoed the same doctrine.) The fines imposed upon rich men for a given offense were much heavier than those imposed upon the poor for the same offense. Lawsuits were heard in courts. Witnesses were required to tell the truth. Liars were severely punished, as were corrupt judges, governors, and tax collectors.

The code suggests a stable and well-organized society, with law and order of great importance. Even the people at the bottom were given some legal protection. "The oppressed," Hammurabi promised, "shall read the writing . . . and he shall find his right."

The empire Hammurabi built was short-lived. He died about 1708 B.C. Almost at once the empire began to fall apart. Revolts erupted, and though his son tried to keep things together, he did not succeed. The northern and southern provinces were soon lost, and the realm shrank to a small territory around the capital city. Around 1600 B.C. the Hittites invaded and destroyed Babylon. Mesopotamia was divided among rival peoples who moved in from every side.

David

You've heard the story of how the young shepherd David killed the Philistine giant Goliath with a stone hurled from his sling? He went on from that victory to become the ruler of the Israelites and founder of a dynasty. The Bible tells us what a great warrior and statesman David was, and a gifted poet too: "the sweet singer of Israel," creator of the Book of Psalms.

It was in the time of the first millennium B.C. that David's dynasty was established. The only evidence we have for it outside the Bible is a fragment of a ninth century B.C. stela, in Aramaic, that refers to the House of David. Yet biblical scholars are agreed that David is not a mythical figure. We will probably never know exactly what happened during the time when David's rule was founded. But the Bible gives us a rich, multihued portrait of David, from youth to old age.

Who was David? And who were his people?

About thirty-five hundred years ago a small band of nomads drifted with their flocks around western Asia. They were aliens, without rights to land or property. They were not homogeneous, but a mixed ethnic group. They moved

9

wherever they could make a living—as shepherds, laborers, slaves, mercenary soldiers. By the time they entered Canaan, a part of what is now Palestine, they were divided into twelve tribes. Wherever they roamed, they were influenced by the cultures of the people they lived among. The Israelites first emerged as a people in the middle of the thirteenth century B.C.

When the Hebrews settled in Canaan they became farmers. They believed in one God, close at hand, who sometimes revealed himself to his people. He raised up prophets for them, seers who could reveal the secrets of the future and guide them in all their concerns.

The Canaanites, who occupied the land when the Jews entered it, lived in small city-states ruled by kings. The Hebrews, by contrast, lived in tribes. At the head of each tribe were the elders. They made the decisions concerning the general welfare of their tribe. There was no government standing above all the tribes. Only rarely did the tribes act together, and then it had to be by agreement of the tribal elders.

Although the Israelites, after the Exodus from Egypt, had conquered Canaan, the victory did not end their struggles with neighboring peoples. There was continual warfare over Canaanite territory. The Israelites' most dangerous enemies were the Philistines, a people solidly entrenched on the low coastlands. (Their name became the basis for the word *Palestine.*) The Israelites found that tremendous stress almost unendurable. A cry for a new and stronger political state arose. "We want a king to create order and unity and provide protection!"

The people turned to the prophet Samuel with a plea to give them a king. At first he resisted, believing the appeal showed a lack of faith in the saving might of God. He warned that if the people placed all power in the hands of one man, they would strip themselves of everything. But the Israelites were so fearful of their enemies that they were willing to take that risk. In the end Samuel yielded, anointing a farmer named Saul as their king. Saul was renowned for his bravery and his great height. After the anointing ceremony, the assembly of the people confirmed that Saul was also the popular choice.

Prophecy set the task of that first king: to fight Israel's enemies and to judge righteously. The king of Israel, unlike many others, was not considered divine, either by nature or by descent. Rather he was an ordinary man, who was inspired to lead by the divine spirit.

Saul collected a small standing army and began surprise attacks to drive the Philistines out of the tribal territory. But it soon turned out that Samuel was not happy with the way Saul led his people. Yet how could he replace him? After all, the king had armed men, and might use them if Samuel acted against him. But the Lord assured Samuel that he had another man in mind, imbued with the divine spirit, who would one day replace Saul.

It was David, the shepherd, whose good looks and magnetic

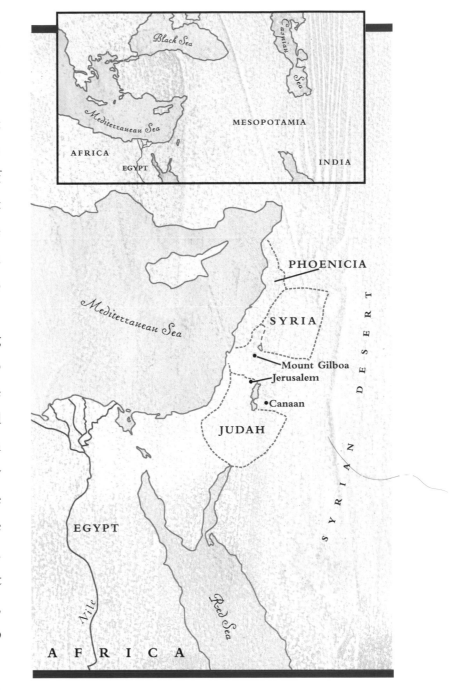

personality would draw people to him. David, a talented musician, entered Saul's service. Saul sensed that he had lost God's favor, and sank into depression and madness. He called on David to soothe his troubled spirit with his skill in playing the eight-stringed lyre. Saul loved him, and made him his armor bearer.

Goliath

Now the Philistines gathered their forces to battle the Israelites. Their troops massed on a hill above one side of a valley, and Saul's soldiers gathered on the hill opposite. Goliath, the champion of the Philistines, a giant with a sword, spear, and huge shield, called to the Israelites: "Send me a man, and we will fight it out in single combat!"

The challenge frightened Saul. He felt he stood no chance against the huge Goliath. Desperate for a champion, he offered great wealth and the hand of his daughter in marriage to any man who would come forth and slay the giant.

David heard Goliath's challenge, and Saul's promise of the great reward for anyone who would defeat the Philistine. "I'm the man," he said. "I'll fight Goliath."

"You can't do that!" cried Saul. "You're only a lad, and he is a veteran soldier!"

"No," David replied, "in my days as a shepherd I protected my flocks from wild beasts, killing any who threatened them. The Lord rescued me from the claws of lion and bear, and he will rescue me from this Philistine!"

And Saul said to David, "Go, and may the Lord be with you."

When Goliath saw a mere youngster approaching him, armed only with a sling and five smooth stones, he laughed. "Come ahead," he said, "and I will carve you up to feed the birds of the air and the beasts of the field."

To which David replied, "You have a sword and a spear and a shield, but I come to you in the name of the God of the armies of Israel! The Lord will deliver you into our power!"

David ran toward Goliath and, putting a stone in his sling, hurled it at the giant, striking him on the forehead and killing him. Then he snatched up Goliath's sword and cut off his head. And when the Philistines saw their champion was dead, they panicked and fled.

David, carrying Goliath's great head, marched along in triumph with Saul, and the women of Israel came out of the towns to greet them, singing

"Saul has killed his thousands,
And David his tens of thousands."

That greater praise of David angered the king, who began to suspect David would one day take his throne away. He tried to humiliate David. Though he had promised his elder daughter to the killer of Goliath, he gave her instead to another man. Then the king's younger daughter, Michal, fell in love with David. But Saul, jealous of David's popularity in the court, put up an obstacle to their marriage. "You can have Michal," he said, "if you go out and slay one hundred Philistines and bring me proof of it." Saul was sure David himself would be killed. To his dismay, David brought back proof he had killed not one hundred but two hundred Philistines. And so Michal became his wife.

David went out on many missions against the Philistines and quickly rose to leadership over elite troops. Whenever he achieved a victory, he grew even more popular with the troops and the people. Saul was all the more certain that David was plotting to take away his throne.

How could he get rid of David? One day, as David was entertaining the court with music, the king in a mad fit suddenly flung his spear at him—and missed. David, knowing he would never again be safe at court, fled into exile, leaving his wife behind. Soon the king had her married to another man. David would remain in exile for a long time.

As the years passed, David became a guerrilla chief. He gathered around him "everyone who was in distress, and everyone who was in debt, and everyone who was discontented." They formed the heart of what grew into a troop of six hundred warriors, fiercely loyal to David. Sometimes they fought alongside the Philistines, helping to overcome tribes that were hostile to both the Israelites and the Philistines. Always they tried to avoid the troops Saul sent out to hunt David down. Meanwhile, in this time when polygamy was quite common, David acquired two new wives. His guerrilla band moved about with a large group of wives and children.

One day the Philistines massed their greatest strength against Saul's weakened kingdom, but luckily told David they did not want his support. (They feared he might switch sides in a battle, and he of course did not want to shed his people's blood.)

The Israelites were defeated in that battle at Mount Gilboa, with Saul and three of his sons killed. The Philistines cut off Saul's head and hammered his body up on a wall. David acted diplomatically by going into mourning for this king who had tried to kill him several times. He even composed an ode to friendship that celebrated the virtues of Saul and his son Jonathan, who had been David's close friend. It was the seed of the tradition that ascribes many psalms to David. His fame as a gifted poet, musician, and composer was deserved, but it is doubtful that he wrote all the seventy-three psalms that are attributed to him.

Now David marched north to Judah, making his home in the old center of his tribe at Hebron. There the elders of Judah chose him to be king. He was thirty years old. One of Saul's generals, however, proclaimed a surviving son of Saul as the true sovereign. A civil war followed, in which both the general and that son died. Their deaths cleared David's path to the throne. About the year 1010 B.C. he was crowned king of all the Israelites.

David's first step was to capture the city of Jerusalem and make it his capital. He had a palace built for himself and quarters for the court. He placed the ancient Ark of the Covenant in a tent near his palace, thereby making Jerusalem the religious, as well as the governmental, center of all Israel. Gradually he created a political system, shaping a nation out of a scattering of tribes. Eventually what had begun as a settlers' colony grew into an empire that filled Palestine and extended into Syria.

The territory he added to his kingdom was rich in copper and iron, invaluable for construction and weaponry. Huge copper and iron smelting furnaces and refineries were manned by slaves or forced labor battalions. David opened up caravan routes that swelled trade with other regions, and built fortresses for defense against the Philistines.

To unify the extensive territory, David created a civil service and placed a scribe at the head of it. Scholars believe it was in David's reign that the recording of biblical history began, a history whose basis was probably the imperial records compiled by the scribal staff. Adding to the records were the findings of a national census that David ordered—not a popular move, for people resented the possibility of being called up for military or labor service.

Though David is esteemed as one of the greatest kings of Israel, he was not without serious flaws. There is the story of David and Bathsheba, told in the Bible. Israel's forces had gone out to battle, while David remained in the palace. One evening he walked on his rooftop to enjoy the cool night air. As he gazed over the city he saw a beautiful woman bathing on her terrace below.

Bathsheba

Desiring her, he sent a messenger to summon her to him. In those ancient times, a woman could not refuse a king's command. She came to him, and they made love.

One day she sent word to David that she was pregnant. To avoid the scandal of a king committing adultery with the wife of one of his soldiers, David moved treacherously against Bathsheba's husband, Uriah. He was away serving with the army. David summoned him home and tried to wheedle him into Bathsheba's bed, so that her baby might seem to be Uriah's child. But when that plan collapsed, David took his cover-up a step further. He ordered what amounted to Uriah's murder. He sent word to Uriah's commander to place him in the front line of the next battle. And there Uriah died.

For that great moral wrong, David was denounced by the prophet Nathan. Conscience-stricken, David begged for forgiveness: "Create in me a clean heart, O God, and renew a right spirit within me." When Bathsheba bore their child, the infant died. After the period of mourning passed, David brought Bathsheba to the palace and made her his wife. She bore him four sons. (One of them, Solomon, became the next king of Israel.)

David was reputed to be the most powerful ruler in the world of his time, the undisputed master of an empire that commanded the most valuable trade routes in the Middle East. The king's merchants sold and transported weapons, chariots, warhorses, and luxury goods to Egypt, Syria, and Mesopotamia. They traded in precious spices with southern Arabia and from there, with the help of Phoenician ships and sailors, reached the ports of Africa and India. Israel's vassal states paid heavy annual tribute, and as the royal treasury swelled, the Israelites' standard of living rose.

To help manage his complex kingdom, David employed foreign experts as well as his own people. He reformed the army. In addition to calling on tribal men in emergencies, he built a regular army, entirely under his command. He made use of war chariots, starting workshops to make the equipment, expanding the stables, and training the charioteers.

Sadly, the man who triumphed in war and diplomacy could not control his own large family. Feuds erupted within it, ending in tragedy several times. As David grew old, one of his sons, the beloved Absalom, the crown prince, rebelled against his father. He gathered supporters and plotted an uprising. David was forced to send troops to put down the rebellion. He gave orders that Absalom's life be spared. But his son lost the battle and his life.

David, a broken man, went from room to room in the palace, grieving for his treacherous son, crying over and over, "Oh, my son Absalom! My son! If only I had died instead of you! Oh, Absalom my son, my son!"

After a forty-year reign over Israel, David died. The Bible says he died "in a good old age, full of days, riches, and honor." True, except for "honor."

Alexander the Great

Picture yourself just finishing your teenage years and setting out to conquer the world.

At twenty, that was what Alexander did. He was the son of Philip II, king of Macedonia, a state in the northern region of ancient Greece. When Philip was assassinated in 336 B.C., Alexander inherited the throne. He launched a career of conquest so brilliant it would make his name a legend through the ages. Alexander the Great, he was called.

When people think of ancient Greece, most probably recall Homer and his epic poems, the *Iliad* and the *Odyssey*, which tell the stories of the Trojan War and the wanderings of the warrior Odysseus in a much earlier time. Scholars believe Homer lived around 800 B.C. The next link to ancient Greece that comes to mind is usually its great classical period, in the fifth century B.C., that golden age of Athens and Greek art.

In the time of Philip and Alexander, the Macedonians were not considered truly Greek by the citizens of such city-states as Athens. They were a tribal people, ruled by a king, while the city-states prided themselves upon their democratic politics (however limited by today's standards). Macedonians didn't speak "proper" Greek and lived more like barbarians than civilized people, it was said. That prejudice made it hard for cooperation to develop between Macedonia and the city-states.

Yet during the reign of Philip, Macedonia became the leading power on the Greek mainland, partly because of his character. He was a brilliant soldier and a fine speaker. He would stop at nothing to attain his goals. He bribed rivals, and killed them if that didn't work, or postponed action until the powerful army he had created could defeat them.

Philip built up his infantry from the hardy and loyal peasants of Macedonia. He recruited his highly trained cavalry from the aristocrats, the land-owning squires.

Philip expanded Macedonia's territory at the expense of his neighbors. He captured a gold mine that yielded him great wealth every year. Then, seeking to rival the Greek city-states to the south in cultural achievement, he built a new capital, Greek-style, at Pella, and invited Greek philosophers and artists to his court.

Philip's queen, Olympias, bore him a son, Alexander, in 356 B.C. There is a famous story about how his young son demonstrated his keenness and his courage. One day Philip was offered a magnificent horse, called Bucephalus. To test the horse before purchase, he had his men try to ride him. Bucephalus proved so savage and unmanageable, rearing up to strike at anyone who came close, that no one could mount him. Disappointed, Philip ordered the horse to be taken away.

Watching this, Alexander said to his father, "They can't handle him because they lack understanding and courage." He kept insisting that he be given a chance to try Bucephalus. Philip was amused. This child criticizing his elders? "You think you know better how to handle a horse?"

"This horse, yes," said Alexander. "I'll manage him better than anyone else would."

"And if you don't? What price will you pay for your rashness?"

"By heaven," said his son, "I shall pay you the price of the horse!"

The king and the courtiers laughed at the boy's nerve. "Done!" said Philip.

Alexander ran to the horse, took hold of the mane, and turned him around to face the sun—realizing, so it seems, that the horse was completely upset by the sight of his own shadow dancing about in front of him.

For a while Alexander trotted alongside the horse, stroking him, then made a flying leap onto his back. The horse, rid of his fear, was eager to race, and Alexander urged him on with a wild cry.

At first Philip was agonized by his son's danger, but when the boy turned

Alexander and Bucephalus

the horse and rode back proudly, the courtiers cheered. Philip wept for joy, kissed his son when he leaped down, and said, "My boy, seek a kingdom to match yourself. Macedonia is not large enough for you."

For one so young, Alexander showed remarkable independence of judgment and keen understanding. These were traits that would earn him many victories in the years ahead.

The Bucephalus story comes from an eyewitness, Marsyas, a classmate of Alexander's at the school of royal pages. About fifty sons of the leading Macedonians attended. At fourteen the boys began a four-year course, graduating at eighteen. Their studies included grammar, logic, arithmetic, geometry, astronomy, music, and, of course, the military arts, such as horsemanship and archery. In their senior year they served in the king's bodyguard in battle. They were trained to be physically fit through athletics, gymnastics, and wrestling. One of Alexander's teachers, Leonidas, became a kind of second father to him. He devised a game in which Alexander played the role of Achilles, the hero of Homer's *Iliad*. The boy saw Achilles as the model of an aristocratic warrior and came to believe he was descended from him.

The year Alexander entered the school, Philip hired Aristotle, one of the most famous philosophers and scientists in the Greek world, to supervise his son's education. There was no major subject of science or philosophy on which Aristotle had not said something worth knowing—cosmography, geography, botany, zoology, medicine. . . . The biographer A. G. L. Hammond writes that above all, Alexander "learned from Aristotle to put faith in the intellect. The boy's admiration developed into a deep affection." The future king undoubtedly was influenced by Aristotle in the decisions he would make that reshaped the world.

Of average height, Alexander had deep-set dark eyes and a mane of dark, curly hair. He didn't see much of his father, who was often away on military campaigns. His mother, Olympias, dominated her son's early years.

By the time Alexander was sixteen, Philip had six wives and several children.

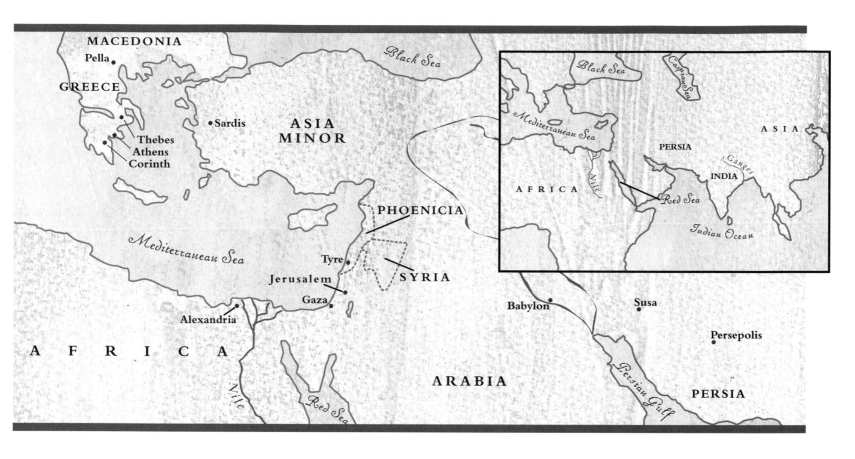

When he went campaigning in Thrace, he left Alexander as his deputy to govern in the capital, Pella. This meant that if the king should be killed, Alexander would be his successor.

By 338, Philip had become master of Greece. That same year Alexander graduated from the royal school, winning honors for his ability as a cavalryman, mounted on his warhorse, Bucephalus.

Alexander's religious faith was a great influence on his career. He worshiped Heracles, the son of the god Zeus, and Achilles, the son of the goddess Thetis. To Alexander these were real people. He hoped to rival or even outdo them as a warrior and a benefactor of humankind. He believed the gods would inspire him in their service.

In the summer of 336, during a festival procession in Macedonia, Philip was assassinated by a young noble. It was never determined what his motive was.

The generals and the troops proclaimed Alexander king. Then something occurred that was not uncommon in contests for power: Alexander killed all others who might claim the throne.

When a son has so extraordinary a father, life must be hard for him. People will compare son with father. Can the son establish his own worth? Will he live in the shadow of his father? If he does not outdo him, he may be laughed at as unequal, as a failure. Here, however, was a son who would outshine his father.

With so young a man as king, some Greek city-states saw it as their chance to get rid of Macedonian domination. Alexander moved too quickly for them. He marched an army south into Greece, and opposition disappeared. At Corinth he was elected captain general of the Hellenic League of city-states, replacing his father in that key position.

Tribes in the north too became troublesome because of Philip's death. Alexander marched against them, punishing those who resisted and making it unquestionably clear that Macedonia still ruled the region. That barely done, he learned that Thebes and Athens were rising against him. They were urged on by Darius III, king of Persia, who offered the cities bribes if they would revolt. Alexander managed to negotiate peace with some cities. But when Thebes refused his offer, he leveled the city, killed the soldiers, and sold the women and children into slavery. He spared only the temples and the house of the poet Pindar. By destroying the city he meant to warn others of what rebellion would cost them. Athens learned the lesson, surrendered, and was treated generously.

With his base in Greece now secure, in 334 B.C. Alexander crossed the Hellespont (today's Dardanelles) into Asia, leading an army of thirty thousand infantry and five thousand cavalry. Behind him he left a trusted general in command of enough troops to assure peace in Macedonia and Greece.

Alexander inherited the finest fighting force the world had yet seen. Both the citizen soldiers and the mercenaries were disciplined and devoted. For the first time in history a scientific analysis of what the men, weapons, and equipment available could do was shaped into the coordinated action of the combined arms. Alexander headed a war machine that could have been successful, say the military experts, "against any other army raised during the next eighteen centuries—in other words, until gunpowder weapons became predominant."

The backbone of the army was the infantry, formed in phalanxes and carrying spears more than thirteen feet long. The foot soldiers were trained to be highly maneuverable, performing in perfect formation. The cavalry, an elite body of upper-class men, were used for shock action. Both Philip and Alexander almost always personally led the cavalry in battle.

The Macedonian army was the first to use prototypes of field artillery. A corps of army engineers ran the siege trains carrying the stone- and bolt-shooting catapults for use in battle and especially in mountain and river crossings. Surgeons attached to the army ran something like a field hospital service.

The army and navy were well paid when on active service. Although military campaigns were very costly, Alexander had the resources: he owned all the mineral deposits, timber stands, and great tracts of land in the kingdom. For outstanding service, men were rewarded with the revenues of an estate, a village, or a harbor.

When Alexander headed for Persia, he had many fewer troops and ships, and much less wealth, than Darius. These facts did not worry this supremely confident young general. Reaching the site of ancient Troy, he prayed, and dedicated his army to the goddess Athena. Marching an average of twenty miles each day, he at last reached the river Granicus. There he met the army of Darius and defeated the Persians. He conquered western Asia Minor and the capital of Darius at Sardis.

What Alexander required of conquered people was the payment of an annual tribute—perhaps a tenth of their production—the supply of troops and labor on demand, and the acceptance of his foreign policy.

The ancient system of intertribal warfare was to be replaced, he hoped, by an era of peace and prosperity. As his armies forged ahead, he would often found new towns, settling a mixed population of Macedonians, Greeks, and the local people. His object was to promote agriculture and trade, and to make

Greek the official language of administration. This policy is what modern scholars have termed Hellenization, and it did much to improve the fortunes of the Greek city-states.

Before Alexander could pursue his enemy into Persia, he had to take control of the seas and the coastal towns of Phoenicia, Palestine, and Egypt. Otherwise his chain of command could be broken. Some places welcomed Alexander, but Tyre resisted. In January 332 he began the siege of that island city. He built a causeway half a mile long to reach it and used ship-borne siege machines to break into its walls. It took seven months to defeat Tyre's army and navy and seize the fortress. Because the Tyrians had slaughtered Macedonians taken prisoner, Alexander treated them harshly. He destroyed most of the city and sold its survivors into slavery.

Greek temple

With his fleets in complete command of the seas in that region, Alexander was able to suppress piracy and to provide protection for the city-states along those shores. Alexander took over rich mineral resources wherever he encountered them, and issued a coinage that became standard in central Europe too.

As he liberated Greek city-states from Persian rule, he got rid of their pro-Persian leadership, brought back exiles, and set up a democracy. When he found that political factions had begun to kill rival factions, he stopped it at once. He realized that if he allowed this to go on, innocents too would be killed—out of personal hatred, or in order to seize their property. He asked for amnesty, the forgiving of political offenses, knowing that without it internal warfare could destroy a community.

One thing that helped Alexander win people to his side was the fact that he banned ravaging and looting. Only rarely did he live off enemy land. Rather, he relied on capturing or buying enemy supplies. When he met resistance, he overcame it by superior power, but did not impose garrisons or demand reprisals.

From Tyre, Alexander marched south. He took Jerusalem. Then, in an assault on the fortified city of Gaza, he was badly wounded in his shoulder by a catapult bolt. He was his own best soldier. This was only one of several times that he was wounded in combat. Despite great loss of blood, he recovered and pushed on into Egypt, which he entered without opposition. The priests and the people, glad to be delivered from Persian domination, welcomed him.

When Alexander made sacrifices to the Egyptian gods, the priesthood recognized him as pharaoh, the supreme ruler, and hailed him as a god. All across the empire oracles had confirmed him as a deity. From this time on he seems to have accepted the idea that he was truly divine.

In Egypt too Alexander promoted Greek culture. In 331 he founded the city of Alexandria. It would become the center of Hellenistic commerce as well as culture. He sent an expedition of scientists up the Nile to determine its sources and to explain the annual flooding of the great river that was so powerful an influence on the history and culture of Egypt.

After several months in Egypt, Alexander moved on to Phoenicia and Syria, hoping for a decisive battle with Darius. The Persian ruler had mustered the finest cavalry of his empire and a huge army of infantrymen. Ready for use was

What do we know about Alexander the Great? And how do we know it?

Those questions lead us to the problem of sources for any historical study. When you read about Hammurabi, king of Babylonia, you find that clay tablets dug up thousands of years after his death provide records of his life and work. In the case of David, king of Israel, portions of the Hebrew Bible tell us his story in considerable detail.

No documents of Alexander's life have been found. The closest we come to his story are accounts written between three and five centuries after his career. One writer, Arrian, says he got his facts from the narratives of Ptolemy and Aristobolus, two generals who campaigned with Alexander. Another contemporary of Alexander was Cleitarchus, upon whose material the historian Plutarch tells us he relied for his life of Alexander. But the original records of those eyewitness sources have not survived.

So when you read about Alexander—and other kings—you have to be aware that later writers looked at their sources with their own biases, their own interpretations of personalities, the values of their own time. And do your best to judge what actually, or probably, happened, and why.

a new weapon, the scythed chariot. It had razor-sharp blades attached to the turning wheels, the chassis, and the yoke pole. Darius believed that a charge by two hundred such two- and four-horse chariots would smash Alexander's famous phalanx formations. On October 1, 331, the two powers met in the battle of Gaugamela. Alexander outmaneuvered the Persians, and Darius panicked and fled. His losses were so great that he would never again raise an imperial army.

Reaching Babylonia, Alexander found rich farmlands, palaces, and treasuries that Darius had abandoned. He moved on to Persepolis, the Persian capital. He shattered its defense force and then exacted retribution for the Persian destruction of Athens in 480. Capturing the citadel, he removed the treasure from it and then rewarded his troops for their hard fighting by letting them loot the palace before they burned it down.

Although Darius was no longer of much account, Alexander wanted to capture him. He caught up with the king only to find that Persian officers had just killed him. Alexander ordered a royal funeral for Darius and now, assuming his crown, began to wear Persian royal clothing and to adopt Persian court ceremonials.

The Macedonians in his army didn't like it when Alexander adopted Asian customs and dress. They liked it even less when he demanded that they prostrate themselves before him. When one of these men plotted against him, Alexander executed the traitor.

What did Alexander know of the geography of the Asia he had set out to conquer? His view of it was derived from the teachings of Aristotle. The scientists of that era, and for many centuries to come, had a limited knowledge of the "inhabitable earth." They thought of it as divided into three areas—Europe, Libya, and Asia—surrounded by a great sea they called Ocean. Aristotle's idea of distance was far more limited than the real dimensions of the globe. Gradually he learned more as the scientists accompanying Alexander sent him reports on distance, climate, geography, flora, fauna, and human and animal ecology.

It was around this time that Alexander sent Aristotle a huge sum of money. With it, Aristotle founded in Athens the first great library of literary texts on papyrus. He also built the first collection of specimens for teaching the natural sciences.

When Alexander decided to move farther into Asia, he mistakenly thought of India as only a small peninsula jutting into Ocean. No problem marching through India to the sea; it was so close! He was wrong, of course. Winning victories along the way, his armies reached the Ganges River. "Enough; stop," the troops cried out. "We've been gone from home far too long; we won't go any farther!" For two days Alexander tried, and failed, to change their minds.

So they turned back. In February 324 Alexander was again in Susa, Persia, which he had left five years earlier. Here he learned that disorder had spread in parts of the empire during his campaigns in the East. Fearing the fall of his empire, he took several steps to reunite it. He ordered eighty of his aristocratic officers to marry Persian princesses. Alexander himself took a daughter of Darius as his second wife. (Earlier, in 327, he had married Rhoxana, the daughter of a Bactrian prince he had captured.) Now he inducted thirty thousand Persian youths into the army, hoping for unification of the troops. This was too much, complained his Macedonians. Persian manners and now Persian troops! Alexander executed thirteen of the rebels and then, in a powerful and moving speech, reminded the army of the glories and honors they had won under his leadership. His words restored their faith in him.

In the spring of 323 Alexander was back in Babylon, where he made plans to explore Arabia and then to invade north Africa. But in June he came down with malaria and suddenly died, at the age of thirty-two. It was just ten years after he had left Macedonia.

The empire fell apart. Alexander's generals competed for power and territory in a multisided conflict that would last for forty years. There was no reconstruction of Alexander's empire. Instead, there emerged a group of large states, each of them a hereditary monarchy. Greek culture continued to spread, with Greek the official language of much of the Middle East. This was especially true in the big cities, where Greek ideas were transmitted. In Alexandria the greatest library of the ancient world was created.

What else Alexander might have achieved in the course of changing history, had he lived longer, can only be guessed. He was a man of strong emotions and brilliant intellect, quick to analyze new situations, both in war and politics, and to devise practical strategies to meet all needs. In his relations with both his own Macedonians and the people he conquered, his powerful personality inspired devotion and loyalty.

In Alexander's time his political vision was unequaled. He had a universal view of humankind: he believed that people should view themselves not merely as citizens of their state while dismissing the rest of humanity as alien; instead, they should regard themselves as part of a global kingdom that embraced all peoples.

The noted military historian Trevor N. Dupuy says of Alexander, "No man in history has surpassed his intellectual, military and administrative accomplishments; not more than two or three are worthy of comparison." Brilliant, visionary, and charismatic, Alexander the Great did indeed live up to his name, as a ruler and as a human being.

Attila

Attila is a powerful if shadowy figure in world history. He was king of the Huns for a brief time in the fifth century. His people were nomads from central Asia. They moved west with their families and their herds of horses during the time when the Roman Empire was falling apart. In one military campaign after another, Attila expanded the Huns' domain till it reached from the Ural Mountains in Russia to the Rhône River in France.

Attila had no real capital. The Huns made the plains of Hungary their nesting ground. From there armies of Huns on horseback would raid in almost every direction to acquire new land, more loot, and greater power, and then return to Hungary.

In many people's minds, Attila was a cruel killer, a bloodthirsty tyrant. And the word *Hun* has come to be a symbol of hate. Down into the twentieth century, when armies devastated an enemy's land, destroyed cities, wiped out populations, it was said they "behaved like Huns."

It is not easy to determine what the truth is. Documentary records are scarce, eyewitness testimony rare and often strongly biased. Historians have not always agreed on their interpretation of Attila's story.

The Huns entered European history at the end of the third century A.D., when they rode from the margins of China across the steppes of western Asia. Entering eastern Europe, they attacked Germanic tribes on the northeastern edge of the sprawling Roman Empire. For a long while they were a loose mixture of scattered nomadic bands, living under chieftains. By the 430s they were molded into a powerful force that dared to attack Germans and Romans alike.

This period was a great turning point in world history. The Middle Ages began with the decline of Rome. The empire's population was dropping and its economy beginning to break down. Its cities—the heart of culture, trade, and communications—slowly shrank. Civil wars within the empire erupted and further weakened its political and economic strength. One territory after another began to separate and withdraw from central control.

The administrative machinery of the state collapsed. The empire became too big for the economy it stood upon. The main goal of imperial taxation was to pay for the military, but it became harder and harder to raise enough money. The result was an army so weakened that it had to recruit the very barbarians it was supposed to hold off. These were mostly Germanic peoples—Goths, Visigoths, Ostrogoths, Vandals, Burgundians, Lombards, Franks, Saxons, Frisians.

By 370 a crisis was developing. The Huns were overrunning one territory after another. And the Germanic peoples they overcame fled farther and farther west. They were enrolled in the empire's armies and served against other barbarians. In 410 a barbarian force, headed by the Visigoth leader Alaric, invaded Rome and sacked the city. It was the first time Rome had been captured by a foreign army.

Why did people migrate in the early Christian era? For several reasons. One was that in the steppe lands of Asia and southeastern Europe, cycles of extreme dryness damaged the fodder upon which the nomads' horses depended. The aridity drove the horse people west in search of new grazing.

The economic resources of nomadic peoples were very meager. They might hunt or fish or forage in the fields for their food. As a warrior people the Huns raided others, near or far, in order to increase their resources through plunder.

The Huns frightened other peoples because of their great skill as warriors.

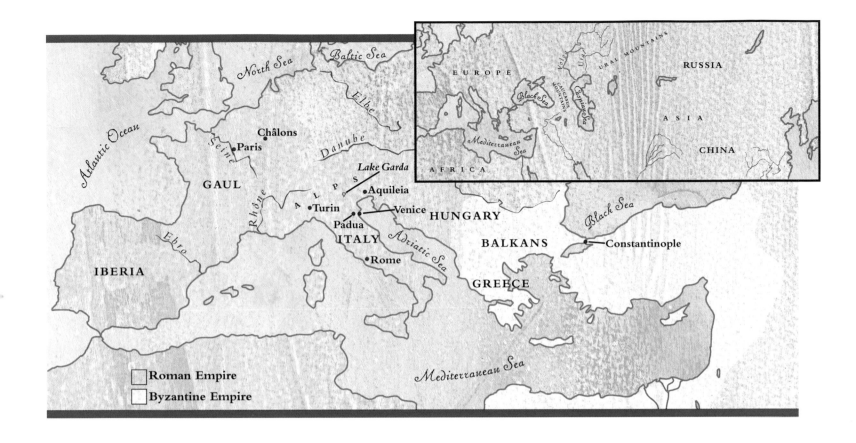

They were superb horsemen and archers. Their breed of horses was superior to other breeds in both speed and endurance. Sixty miles per day was routine for them. One Roman observer noted that though the Huns' horses looked ugly, that was "set off by their fine qualities—sober nature, cleverness and their ability to endure any injuries as well."

Boys learned to ride, it seems, about as soon as they learned to walk. The Huns were so at ease on horseback that they could sleep while riding. Horse and rider must be nailed together, said one observer. Hun warriors always traveled with a string of horses to make sure they had a fresh one when needed.

The Huns developed bows so powerful that they could fire arrows a distance of one hundred thirty yards and could kill a man at half that distance. Their arrows were made of wood strengthened with bone inlays. In battle warriors would carry thirty arrows each in their quivers. Behind them rode workmen with additional supplies of arrows in case more were needed.

A striking force of Hun warriors numbered between five hundred and one thousand men. Patrick Howarth, Attila's biographer, wrote that they engaged the enemy "by firing arrows at a distance of about one hundred thirty yards. They would advance in a zigzag fashion, pretend to withdraw, then advance again. Standing in their stirrups, they could fire their arrows forward, backward or sideways. . . . Surprise and terror were the essence of Hun tactics. Their whole strategy was, in a number of respects, a forerunner of the twentieth century blitzkrieg."

As they moved into territory of the Roman Empire, the Huns confronted many peoples. Some they fought with; some accepted rule by the invaders. Others became refugees, and still others entered the Hun armies. In this early period there was no united command. One group of Huns would ride off in one direction while another headed elsewhere.

war arrows

To forestall invasion, Roman emperors tried to buy off the Huns. They made agreements to send them annual tribute in gold. They concluded it was better to lose gold than to lose men in battle. They knew that plunder was what the Huns wanted. And much of the gold paid them would be spent in buying goods from the empire. So why not make a commercial deal that would benefit both sides?

A common practice of the Huns was to capture hostages. They often held the young sons of powerful Romans hostage as a way of applying pressure for a deal. It frequently worked.

In 434 Attila's father, Ruga, died, leaving the kingdom to his two sons, Attila and his older brother, Bleda.

In 441 Attila began his first invasion of the Eastern Roman, or Byzantine, Empire. He led his Huns to the walls of Constantinople, almost wiping out the imperial army, and then ranged over the Balkans almost at will. Finally the emperor Theodosius decided peace was best and pledged a tribute of gold to Attila.

In 443 Bleda died: a hunting accident, some said. It was more widely believed that Attila had arranged his brother's murder. Now he was the sole ruler of a vast empire. It ranged from southern Germany in the west to the Volga River or the Ural River in the east, and from the Baltic Sea in the north to the Danube River, Black Sea, and Caucasus Mountains in the south.

Attila then tried a second invasion of the Eastern Empire. Constantinople panicked at the danger, especially because its walls had just been shattered by an earthquake. The walls were hastily rebuilt, and Attila lacked the power to break them down. Disease—probably malaria and dysentery—had badly weakened his troops. Nevertheless the Huns were still a serious threat, and Attila's demands for even greater tribute were met by the emperor's imposing heavy taxation on the rich. Constantinople realized that so long as Attila remained alive, there could be no lasting peace.

Now Attila turned his army away from Constantinople and headed toward Greece. Greece and the Balkan provinces soon proved to be rather poor pickings: the region had been so often fought over that there was little wealth of any kind left there. Attila, deciding that greater opportunities could be found in Gaul (modern France and Belgium) and Spain, headed west. In 451 he crossed the Rhine River leading a great army of some one hundred thousand warriors. Traveling with them were a large wagon train of supplies and many Hun families. The main body of his army were Hun cavalrymen, but there were also large detachments of others. They moved on a front more than one hundred miles wide, sacking most of the towns of northern Gaul.

Legend has it that the city of Paris itself was saved by the divine interven-

Though taking pride in his origins as a Hun, Attila knew his people had much to learn from more advanced cultures. As Peter the Great of Russia would do more than a thousand years later, Attila tried to raise the standards of his kingdom to the level of cultures he observed elsewhere. He wanted to deal with great kings as their equal. He drew into his circle of advisers several educated foreigners. They spoke either Latin, the common tongue of the Western Roman Empire, or Greek, the language of the Eastern Empire. The Huns probably spoke a Turkic language; they were without writing, so we cannot be sure.

Their religion was a form of nature worship. Animals played a part in it, just as they did in everyday life. Horses were sacrificed as offerings to a deity. Horse skulls were placed on poles in front of homes to keep off evil. When the dead were buried, swords—so highly valued by a warrior people—were placed in the graves.

That the Huns were fine craftspeople is proved by the objects found in their graves. They made beautiful bridles and saddles as well as swords and bows and arrows. Gold was central to their decorative arts. They collected much of it in the form of plunder or tribute. In Hungary museum visitors can see relics of the Huns' warrior life.

Like most people of their time, the Huns enslaved many of those they conquered, selling off those they did not want for themselves. In the territory they controlled they used slaves as agricultural workers or as soldiers. Some military units had as many slaves as free men.

In their migrations the Huns encountered numerous other peoples. And as always happens in such circumstances, they intermarried. So as the generations passed, it became harder and harder to determine who was distinctively a Hun. From the mingling of many peoples new human groups emerge, carrying the traits of their forebears.

tion of Saint Genevieve. At the age of seven, Genevieve had been persuaded by a bishop to dedicate herself to a life of faith. After her parents died, she came to Paris and soon became known for her good deeds. When rumors spread that the Huns were coming to destroy Paris, she called upon the people not to abandon the city—and Attila turned away.

Christian chroniclers of that time held that whenever cities suffered destruction, it was as a punishment for the sins of the people. When destruction and death did not occur, it was because of divine response to prayers and the good conduct of believers. Attila was seen as heaven's instrument for the punishment of the sinful. That is why he was called the Scourge of God.

After devastating northern France, Attila moved south to meet a large Gallo-Roman army. A great battle took place at Châlons. The fighting was fierce but the ending was uncertain. Both sides suffered frightful losses. Military historians say that Châlons, fought in 451, was one of the crucial battles of world history. If Attila had clearly won, it could have meant the complete collapse of remaining Roman civilization and Christian religion in western Europe, and perhaps domination of Europe by an Asian people.

Speculation, of course. No one really knows. Historians are not fortune-tellers. At any rate, Attila and his army returned to Hungary.

What did the Huns' king look like? How did he strike people who knew him? We have only the testimony of one man who saw him, spoke with him, and left a record of his impressions. He was Priscus, a Greek-speaking Roman citizen. He tells us that Attila was short and stocky in build, with a large head and a skimpy beard. He had deep-set eyes, a flat nose, and swarthy skin. To the aristocratic Priscus all Huns were "barbarians," yet he observed Attila to be a loving father who lived plainly and earned the loyalty of his close associates. In sum, he wrote, this was "a man to shake the world."

Half a century before, the Visigoth army under Alaric had marched on Rome and besieged the empire's capital. Alaric had withdrawn only when paid an immense ransom in gold, silver, silks, and spices. Attila thought he was an even greater general. Why couldn't he take Rome and gain even more loot? In 452 he crossed the Alps into northeastern Italy, taking Turin and Padua. His next goal was to conquer Aquileia, a major city at the head of the Adriatic Sea. It was a fortress as well as a great commercial center, and in the past had blocked invaders. It was months before Attila's troops were able to break through the walls and capture the city. And they destroyed it, to set an example for other cities to learn from.

Was that worse than what others have done? It was just what the Roman armies had done in the days of the Republic when they reduced Carthage to ruins. And think of World War II and what air raids did to Dresden, and nuclear bombs to Hiroshima and Nagasaki.

As Attila advanced, the people of the region withdrew to the islands off the coast, where only fishing villages existed. It was this influx that led to the founding of the city of Venice.

Famine and disease were raging in Italy, so Attila had great trouble collecting supplies for his men and horses. Would he be able to continue his march on Rome? At this time a delegation from Rome, headed by Pope Leo I, visited the Huns' camp on the shores of Lake Garda. Their task was to persuade Attila not to attack Rome. No one knows for certain what was said. But Attila did turn back, and Rome was spared.

Was it because the pope offered tribute to Attila if he would withdraw? Or was Attila awed by the majesty of the pope in his pontifical robes? Perhaps Attila simply feared that his line of communications was insecure and his army in danger because of the pestilence. One story holds that during his conference with the pope, Saint Peter and Saint Paul appeared alongside Leo and threatened Attila with instant death should he deny the pope's request. (That scene was painted by Raphael and appears on a wall of the Vatican.) At any rate, Attila did withdraw, and history accords Leo I the credit for it.

By the spring of 453 Attila was back in Hungary. Although he already had many wives, he fell in love with a young and beautiful woman. Their wedding was celebrated with a great party at the palace. Late in the evening the bride and groom retired to their room. When Attila did not appear the next morning, his courtiers were alarmed and broke into the bedroom. They found Attila dead and his new wife weeping behind her veil. It was said that Attila had burst an artery while lying prone and was suffocated by a torrent of blood.

Where he was buried is not known. His tomb was probably filled with gold and silver ornaments. Archaeologists have never found the burial place.

Attila's was a short reign—only eight years. In that time he forced rulers in both the Eastern and Western Empires to pay him huge amounts of ransom. Kings, emperors, and generals all feared and respected him.

After Attila's death his three sons quarreled over the distribution of power. Their factional fights weakened the Hun military, and what was left of Attila's empire soon disintegrated. The Huns continued in the pages of history only as mercenaries in the armies of eastern and central Europe.

The name and reputation of Attila were revived in centuries to come when composers such as Verdi and Wagner, dramatists, and filmmakers created operas, plays, and movies drawing upon Attila's legendary exploits. In the 1990s a Hungarian composer even created a rock opera called *Attila*. In modern Hungary Attila's name is much respected, and children are often named after him.

Charlemagne

History knows him as Charlemagne, or "Charles the Great," one of the legendary figures of the Middle Ages. He was a rare combination of warrior and scholar. As warrior he battled to extend the boundaries of his Christian kingdom on all sides. He started as king of the Franks and made himself emperor of the West. He founded the Holy Roman Empire and stimulated the economic and political life of Europe.

As scholar he mastered Latin and could speak it as well as his native tongue. He studied the liberal arts and fostered education and a cultural renaissance.

There is little known about Charlemagne's childhood and youth. The sources are thin. His only biography by someone who knew him was written by the abbot Einhard a decade after the king's death. But he gives us few of the details of his subject's life and times, perhaps because he had no contemporary biographies on which to model his work. No one had written such personal histories for some five hundred years, not since the time of the Roman Empire.

Einhard's biography was colored by his desire to make Charlemagne and his dynasty look good. Luckily there are other documentary records that modern historians have used, annals kept by monks in monasteries. These writings provide detailed accounts of events during the reign of Charlemagne. Then too there are collections of saints' lives. They offer insights into the religion and politics of the period.

Charlemagne was the grandson of Charles Martel, who gained control of Aquitaine, a large region of today's France. Charlemagne's father, Pépin III, made himself the first king of a new Frankish dynasty. Pépin and his wife, Bertrada, had two sons, Charles and Carloman. Upon Pépin's death in 768, the two brothers ruled jointly, each responsible for a different part of the realm. Inevitably rivalry arose that threatened to bring on civil war, but then Carloman suddenly died. Charlemagne was left as sole ruler of the entire kingdom of the Franks.

The Franks were a Germanic people who originally lived along the Rhine River. Together with other Germanic groups, around A.D. 200 they began moving into the territory of the declining Roman Empire. Roman ways attracted their chieftains, as well as the prospect of loot and of paid service with the Roman army. Sometimes the Romans enrolled whole tribes as mercenaries to serve against other tribes.

The Franks, a warrior society, settled within areas now part of Belgium and France. Their territory became known as Francia. One of their earliest kings, Clovis, embraced Christianity, giving the Franks the support of the Church.

The Frankish nation developed into something more than a collection of barbarian war bands. The war bands became a people belonging to a recognizable state, although different groups of the empire still spoke different languages and could communicate only in Latin. These of course were the literate ones. The pagan beliefs that many Franks clung to were gradually reconciled with Christianity.

Most people living in Francia were scarcely aware of inhabiting a nation or a state. They were intensely local in view, more interested in their neighbors and the goings-on in the next village than in differences between their state and others in Europe. "Europe" itself was still only a dim concept, which few thought about or grasped. Even upper-class people had a limited knowledge of the world, depending upon maps drawn on parchment. These pictured the

world map

world as a flat disc divided into three continents—Asia, Africa, and what came to be called Europe. Christendom? Most were only vaguely conscious of being part of a far-spreading religious community. The word *Europe* would not be applied to western Christendom until the tenth century, long after Charlemagne's time.

When Charlemagne became sole ruler, he moved against those who threatened his power. To expand his territory he defeated one rival, the king of the Lombard people of northern Italy, and had himself crowned king in his place. Then he forged an alliance with the papacy, glad to have the pope's protection. Thus he took control of a large part of Italy, which brought new wealth and peoples into his growing empire.

Before he was through with the Lombards, Charlemagne declared war against the pagan Saxons, another Germanic people. (They had begun moving into the old Roman province of Britain from the fourth century onward.) For thirty years Charlemagne hammered away at the Saxons. He would kill thousands of them in a single day without a quiver of conscience. Charlemagne's policy was an early example of the enforced Christianization of people considered to be "barbaric" or "primitive."

While still struggling to subdue the Saxons, who often revolted, Charlemagne waged other campaigns to broaden his empire. Best remembered is his expedition into Spain, for in 778 something happened there that is commemorated in literature. Part of his army, led by Count Roland, was ambushed by Basques near Roncesvalles, and Roland was killed. The epic poem *The Song of Roland* tells the story. The outcome of the campaign was the establishment of a militarized buffer zone between Frankish land and Muslim Spain.

Marching to his eastern frontier, Charlemagne defeated the duke of Bavaria, adding that duchy to his empire. Farther east was the huge Slavic territory held by an Asiatic people, the Ayars. Charlemagne smashed their power in four years of assault and made their kingdom a tributary state.

By 800 Charlemagne could map a vastly extended empire. It ran from the Elbe River in Germany to south of the Pyrenees in Spain and from the North Sea to southern Italy. His authority rivaled that of the old Roman emperors at the peak of their power.

In Rome the papacy moved to proclaim how much it valued Charlemagne's protection and political leadership. He had brought all the invaders of the Roman lands within a single faith. True, he had often imposed conversion at the point of a sword. But that was how power was practiced at that time. On Christmas Day of the year 800, Pope Leo III crowned Charlemagne the Holy Roman Emperor.

Under Charlemagne Christianity was preached everywhere, and the Church and its institutions were encouraged. But the ancient faiths rooted in the past could not be wiped out overnight. The history of the Church shows constant combat with older beliefs even into modern times. Paganism survived

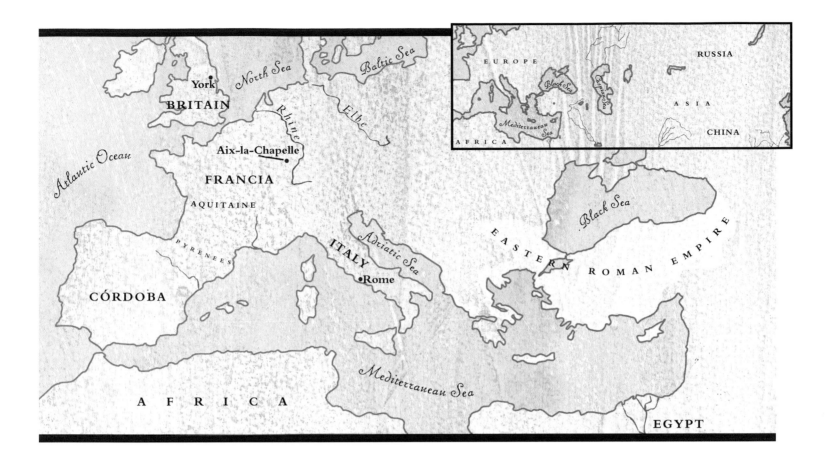

in many places, along with magicians, enchanters, sorcerers, dream interpreters, astrologers, and fortune-tellers. Though Charlemagne condemned it, belief in witchcraft persisted, at great cost especially to women. Many were persecuted, even burned alive, on the charge of witchery.

What was Frankish society like at that time? Francia was a world of forest and wasteland with villages and lords' manors scattered here and there. Towns were just beginning to grow and commerce to revive.

Travel in those times, whether local or distant, was always dangerous. The roads were not safe. Thieves were everywhere. Outlaws hid in the forests, leaping out to rob passersby. They even dogged the army, hoping to pillage the baggage carts. Charlemagne's penalties were harsh for all forms of thievery: for a first offense, loss of an eye; for a second, slitting of the nostrils; for a third, execution.

Everyday life was brutal too. When people quarreled, ears were cut off, eyes torn out, noses slit, tongues ripped out, teeth broken, joints crushed, hands and feet amputated, testicles smashed. Punishment for such "misbehavior" was just as harsh: mutilation, castration, burning, drowning.

Charlemagne

47

Charlemagne tried to prevent feuds that could kill entire families. When civil wars broke out, the devastation was terrible—slaughter, or mass deportation of men, women, and children.

Fear and insecurity drove people, both the lofty and the humble, to seek protection and sustenance from one another. Everyone looked to their neighbors and above all to God and his angels and saints for aid and comfort. It was a struggle to live yet another day against the threat of famine, disease, and violence.

People commonly died at what we today would think a very early age. Infant mortality was high. Famine came often, at one time taking a third of the population. A survivor of a famine in 793 wrote that "some welcomed the hungry into their houses, killed them, and put the bodies into the salt tub. . . . Men ate men, brothers ate brothers, and mothers their children." Epidemics took further deaths, while the malnutrition that followed piled the dead even higher. There were no medicines of the modern kind to ease or cure illness. But every monastery had its herb garden and infirmary for the care not only of its ailing members but also the local sick. If the medicinal herbs did not work, one could only pray and wait for the end.

The unfree had no rights. Their master had complete power over them. Slavery was still common, for the many wars of conquest kept the institution alive. Slaves were sold within the empire or abroad. Slaves worked on the land or as artisans in the towns.

The rural folk made up four fifths of the population. They might own a small farm or work for others as tenants or farm laborers. Free men could acquire ownership of land by developing it out of uncultivated wasteland. They lived in houses built of wood or stone—whatever was at hand.

The upper class dominated society. A small group who succeeded in gaining power by force or through diplomacy, these aristocrats controlled the sources of wealth and held the key civil and religious positions. The father in such an aristocratic family was all-powerful.

The aristocrats married into one another's families, thereby adding to their power. They held immense wealth in land, acquired by conquest, gift, or purchase, as well as by marriage. Some families had many large estates in several parts of the empire. In their relations with the king, the aristocrats played the double role of counselors and faithful followers.

These landed gentry were the heart of the military. The king depended upon them for his cavalry and to pay for costly arms and equipment. The price of a horse and sword, for instance, might be as high as the value of both a farm and a slave. A knight had not only to equip himself, but to provide horse and arms for his squire, provisions for three months of campaigning, and more.

Boys born into the aristocracy were destined for war. Drummed into them was the sure knowledge that they would have to be able to withstand hardship, hunger, cold, heat, and the risks of combat. At about fourteen a boy was handed a sword by his father, a token of his entry into the adult world. The sword—and his horse—became his lifetime companions.

If aristocrats yearned for combat, not so the bulk of the army. These were the infantrymen, who saw no glamour or romance in warfare. They hated to leave their families and the farmwork, and couldn't wait to return home to bring in the harvest and the vintage. Among the infantry desertion was common, with death the penalty.

Estimates vary on the size of Charlemagne's army; the lower guess is about three thousand cavalry and ten thousand infantry. In enemy territory the troops relished the prospect of looting. They ferreted out anyone alive to sell as slaves and stole sheep and cattle and produce. Everything they couldn't carry off they put to the torch.

How did Charlemagne govern his empire?

The emperor's responsibility was to keep the peace. Within the kingdom, not beyond it, where he fought many wars of both defense and offense. He was responsible too for administering justice. This function he delegated to the nobles in charge of the many districts of the empire. He instructed them to "do justice fairly, correctly, and equitably to churches, widows, orphans, and all others, without fraud, corruption, obstruction or abusive delay, and be vigilant that all your subordinates do likewise."

What did Charlemagne look like? And what was his character? Our only personal report comes from his friend Einhard's Life of Charlemagne:

Charles was large and strong and of lofty stature, though not disproportionately tall (his height is well known to have been seven times the length of his foot); the upper part of his head was round, his eyes very large and animated, nose a little long, hair fair, and face laughing and merry. Thus his appearance was always stately and dignified, whether he was standing or sitting, although his neck was thick and somewhat short and his belly rather prominent; but the symmetry of the rest of his body concealed these defects. His gait was firm, his whole carriage manly, and his voice clear, but not so strong as his size led one to expect. . . .

He used to wear the national, that is to say the Frank, dress: next to his skin a linen shirt and linen breeches and above these a tunic fringed with silk, while hose fastened by bands covered his lower limbs, and shoes his feet; and he protected his shoulders and chest in winter by a close-fitting coat of otter or marten skins. Overall he flung a blue cloak, and he always had a sword girt about him, usually one with a gold or silver hilt and belt; he sometimes carried a jeweled sword, but only on great feast days or at the reception of ambassadors from foreign nations. He despised foreign costumes, however handsome, and never allowed himself to be robed in them, except twice in Rome. . . .

Charles had the gift of ready and fluent speech, and could express whatever he had to say with the utmost clearness. He was not satisfied with command of his native language merely, but gave attention to the study of foreign ones, and in particular was such a master of Latin that he could speak it as well as his native tongue; but he could understand Greek better than he could speak it. . . . He most zealously cultivated the liberal arts, held those who taught them in great esteem, and conferred great honors upon them. . . . The King spent much time and labor . . . studying rhetoric, dialectics, and especially astronomy; he learned to reckon, and used to investigate the motions of the heavenly bodies most curiously, with an intelligent scrutiny. He also tried to write, and used to keep tablets and blanks in bed under his pillow, that at leisure hours he might accustom his hand to form letters; however, as he did not begin his efforts in due season, but late in life, they met with ill success.

He cherished with the greatest fervor and devotion the principles of the Christian religion, which had been instilled into him from infancy.

The leading landowners were his chief counselors, judges, and administrators. They met in annual assemblies, numbering hundreds of men, in the spring. Here new laws were proposed and military objectives considered. The nobles had to produce the armies needed to achieve the agreed-upon goals. We have no evidence to indicate how democratic these assemblies were. It would seem that some degree of consensus had to be achieved. If not, revolt might threaten.

Of course there was time for fun and games. What aristocrat could do without them? Sports were a major outlet, with hunting the favorite. The rich kept reserves of wild animals and even menageries.

Eating—that was a major concern: food, and lots of it, especially roasted meats. The kitchens smoked day and night, and the head cook was a palace favorite. Charlemagne himself was a notoriously big eater. The more food laid out, the greater a royal's prestige. Musicians entertained the guests on their lyres and zithers while mimes made the dining hall rock with laughter. Wine was drunk every day. Every class of society drank too much, with abbots and bishops setting the example. If wine was not at hand, then beer would do, but that was considered a penance. Water supplies were often unsafe to drink. However, wine and beer kept without refrigeration for long periods, and they were often drunk at less than full strength. Few other beverages were available.

Both the royal villas and the great monasteries had their corps of artisans: blacksmiths, goldsmiths, saddlers, carpenters, parchment makers. . . . The aristocrats valued artisans who could make the luxury products they loved, and sculptors, painters, and goldsmiths enjoyed a special place. Many objects were made of wood, for iron was scarce. The blacksmiths were much in demand; they were depended upon for weaponry.

Although much of the economy was local, trade did exist, carried on by merchants. They might be simply peddlers, selling in local markets, or they could be international traders. These last, on their own or working for aristocrats, abbots, or princes, transported goods by cart or boat from one corner of the empire to another. Products moved back and forth between the West and Asia and Africa. A merchant might carry bearskins, marten fur, swords, and eunuchs from Francia to sell in Egypt, or cinnamon, musk, aloes, wood, and camphor from the Orient to sell in the West.

When Charlemagne's armies raided Slavic lands, they opened up a new supply of slaves. At one time a monk recorded observing six ships in an Italian port filled with nine thousand slaves heading for a market in Egypt. The emir of Córdoba in Spain bought five thousand slaves to staff his army, his administration, and his harem.

Charlemagne had many royal residences. Clustered around each were peasants, artisans, clerks, and other functionaries. He traveled much with his court, moving from one estate to another, staying now for a day or two, or perhaps a few months. The rural residences were nothing elegant, and almost all have disappeared.

But in 794 Charlemagne decided to enlarge his modest palace at Aix-la-Chapelle, now Aachen in Germany, into a truly imperial palace and make it the political center of his empire. It became a vast collection of buildings surrounded by a four-gated wall. Nearby were the homes of bishop and abbot and other dignitaries such as his friend Einhard. Charlemagne dearly loved to swim and bathe in the thermal springs at Aix-la-Chapelle. He spent the last years of his life in this city and is buried in his chapel there, in its day the largest stone building north of the Alps.

To Charlemagne, one of his most important missions was to lead his people to salvation. He believed that the rural folk, the artisans, the merchants must be instructed in the Christian religion. And the newly conquered pagan peoples had to be converted. It would take well-educated teachers to do all this.

The king ordered that schools be established where children would learn reading, the psalms, chanting, computation, and grammar. Parchment books had to be carefully copied and placed in classrooms. Schools became major responsibilities of bishops and abbots.

It was believed that a child in the sixth year was ready for schooling. Parents could offer their sons or daughters to the Church for education, binding the child to the monastic life permanently. The education was free. Most monks and almost all nuns were recruited from the upper class. In the monasteries their time was given to both intellectual and manual labor, with only an hour per month, or maybe per week, for free time in which to relax.

Charlemagne himself knew how to read and was quite learned. But he never mastered writing. Writing was a difficult skill practiced only by specialists in those days.

A child completing the first studies would take up the liberal arts as part of secondary education. These included arithmetic, geometry, astronomy, and music. The subjects were not ends in themselves, but steps to the highest level: philosophy or Christian theology.

It wasn't only clerks and monks who were schooled. Lay aristocrats too wanted to be educated as a measure of their breeding. Mothers were more concerned than fathers that this be done. Men preferred to see their sons as expert riders, warriors, and hunters rather than as scholars.

The end results of Charlemagne's educational program went beyond its initial aim. It led to a kind of literary renaissance. Contributing to it were many scholars that he brought in from abroad—Spanish, English, Irish, Italian. One of them, Alcuin, a Saxon from York, became a longtime close friend and adviser of the king and took charge of several abbeys.

These strangers influenced the cultural life of both church and lay leaders, as well as of Charlemagne's own children, both boys and girls. The scholars explored serious problems in continued discussions. They were responsible for thousands of manuscripts that have been preserved and for the adoption of a more readable and regular minuscule hand, which the printers of the future would adapt in their lowercase typography.

The image of Charlemagne was transfigured by legend. One story held that when his tomb was opened in the year 1000 Charlemagne was found "seated on a throne as if he still lived." He was often portrayed with a flowing white beard, which it seems he never actually wore.

That he was dynamic and brilliant is certain, and that he had a firm belief in his mission to uphold and propagate Christianity by sword or book. His reign helped bring to birth a new European society.

Kublai Khan

Look for Asia on a map of the world—and see how huge it is. It's the biggest of the world's seven continents. Even bigger than North America and South America put together.

Now find the country of Mongolia in Asia. It sits in the center of the continent. North of it is the Siberian portion of Russia, and east, south, and west of it is China. Mongolia is landlocked; it has no coastline. In area, Mongolia is slightly larger than Alaska. It is a desolate windswept land, where today horses outnumber humans two to one. The sparse population is concentrated in the grasslands of the northern part. Below that region is the great and forbidding Gobi Desert.

Yet in the twelfth and thirteenth centuries, under Genghis Khan and his grandson Kublai Khan, the Mongols ruled an empire that stretched from the China Sea in the east to the far-distant European country of Hungary in the west. The Mongols created the largest continuous land empire in the history of the world.

How did that happen? How could a people so small in number come to dominate so large a part of the world?

Kublai Khan was the sovereign ruler of that vast empire at its peak. (The word *khan* means "sovereign" or "king.") Most of Kublai's people lived in the central or steppe region of Mongolia. There was just enough water and grass to support a pastoral economy, but not intensive agriculture.

The Mongols relied on five basic animals: sheep, goats, and yaks for food, clothing, shelter, and fuel; camels for desert transport; and horses for cavalry warfare and for a kind of "pony express" postal system. It was a hazardous nomadic life, always at risk from drought, harsh winters, and diseases afflicting their animals. In so fragile an economy they had to rely on obtaining grain from China in exchange for animals and animal products.

In the late twelfth century the Mongol tribes, led by military chieftains and nobles who owned large herds, dominated the land. It was Genghis Khan (c. 1162–1227) who united the diverse tribes and organized them into a powerful army. He proved to be a military genius capable of challenging sedentary civilizations and bringing them under his control.

He convinced his people that the sky god had made him responsible for unifying the Mongols and ruling the world. They must be ready to ride out of their homeland to conquer other territories.

The Mongols were horse warriors; they were always ready to move, fast and anywhere. Settled people—farmers—found it much harder to do that. "The ancient nomads of the arid steppe," says the military historian John Keegan, "must have been the toughest people in creation."

You might ask why the nomads didn't settle down in gentler climates where cultivated land could provide a steady supply of food. The answer is that they loved the nomadic way of life. They looked on the tired farmer with contempt. Farm people were bound fast to their plows and their oxen. They never went anywhere. Nomads wanted their free life with its horses, their tented camps, their hunts, their seasonal shifts of quarters. And if you could have the comfort and luxury of settled peoples by conquering them and exacting tribute, why not enjoy the best of both worlds?

In their early military campaigns the Mongols headed toward China. It was

Great Wall

to fend off the Mongols, and other invaders from north of the Yellow River, that Chinese emperors began to build the Great Wall. If that primary line of defense was penetrated, they counted on the superiority of Chinese civilization to induce the "barbarians" to reach some way of accommodation. That policy worked for more than a thousand years—until Genghis Khan, starting in 1211, began to overrun much of China very quickly.

Kublai Khan

After completing the conquest of northern China, the Mongols turned west. Their armies poured into Russia. They captured Kiev and the lower Volga River region and then raided farther into Europe. The Teutonic Knights, the Poles, and the Hungarians all lost to the invaders. The Mongols had reached into Croatia and Albania when they were recalled home by the death of Genghis. They were so successful in the west possibly because there was no great single power to stand up to them; they faced divided enemies.

The military success of Genghis and, later, his grandson Kublai, stunned their world. The Mongol armies struck with the speed and force of a tornado. Because their victories were so swift and sure, their victims would say that they had been beaten only because of overwhelming numbers. Not true. The Mongol armies usually were smaller than those of their opponents. They rarely ran to more than 150,000 men, and often far fewer.

It was quality, not quantity, at the core of their success. The Mongol troops were the best-trained soldiers of their time, highly skilled in the use of weapons. Their chief battle weapons were the bow, the battle-ax, the javelin, and the lasso. Each cavalryman carried two quivers of arrows, with additional ones close by in a supply train. And each trooper had the use of spare horses herded behind the column.

Battlefield coordination of all the units, from the largest to the smallest, was precise, the outcome of intense training. The mobility of the Mongol armies has rarely been equaled. They operated on the basic principle of seizing and maintaining the initiative.

When the Mongol cavalry first attacked the Chinese, they came up against the strong walls of Chinese cities. But within a few years intense study of the problem led to the adoption of Chinese weapons, equipment, and techniques. The khans developed a system of assault upon fortifications that would rarely fail them. They conscripted the best Chinese engineers and built an engineering corps said to be as good as those of Alexander the Great and Julius Caesar. Almost no fortification could withstand their assault.

Genghis and Kublai were different from earlier nomad warlords. They were not out for loot or settlement. They fired their people with a divine mission of conquest. What they vanquished, they usually did not destroy. They set about organizing the territory in a systematic way. Kublai was open to other civilizations and respectful of religions other than his own paganism—Islam, Christianity, Buddhism. He valued what the wise men of other cultures had to offer. If their experience and their ideas would help, he'd use them.

But what made the Mongol campaigns so successful? Not superior technology. Yet most of the people they attacked surrendered without a fight. Why?

Military historians conclude that one big factor was the widespread reputation of the Mongols as an unbeatable army. Kublai Khan, like his grandfather, enforced a powerful discipline on his warriors: all booty must be held collectively. Any soldier who abandoned a comrade in battle must be executed.

No campaign was fought without intense preparation. A broad network of spies operating in the guise of merchants or traders brought back every scrap of information about the intended victims. And above all this, a fiery nationalism imbued the Mongols with the belief that they were a chosen people who couldn't lose.

But let's not forget the power of terror. Stories about Mongol barbarity and ruthlessness spread everywhere. There was some truth to them. If the defenders of a fortress or city defied the Mongols and tried to hold out against them, the khan's army, when it breached the walls, exacted punishment by killing or enslaving the losers and destroying their city. There was no attempt to conceal these facts. The Mongols deliberately let the world know what they had done. Their aim was to discourage resistance by the next victim on the list.

What helped mightily was the fact that the Mongols were generous with any foe who showed readiness to cooperate. When there was little or no armed resistance, the Mongols created what one historian has called "the most carefully planned military government system to appear before the twentieth century." They selected a local leader to conduct the civil government. He was supported and supervised by a Mongol occupation force. They wisely chose not to let conquered territories become a burden on the Mongol economy. The taxes they collected were used to maintain local government and the occupation troops—and of course to pay tribute to the Mongol capital.

Quarreling among local factions was strictly forbidden, and law and order were insisted upon. As a result regions occupied by the Mongols were often much more peaceful than before the invasion.

Genghis Khan died in 1227. He was buried in northeast Mongolia. Forty young women and forty horses were sacrificed at his tomb. He left a vast territory to his descendants, but no sure indication of who would succeed him in leadership. Eventually his third son became the supreme ruler of the Mongol lands. When he died, in 1241, Kublai (whose father had been passed over as the heir to Genghis) began to gain prominence.

Kublai was born in 1215, as Mongol expansion was beginning under Genghis. His mother, Sorghaghtani Beki, was a brilliant woman whom one Persian historian of her time said "towered above all the women in the world." She was the niece of a Mongol tribal chief, married to Tolui, a son of Genghis who was often away from home on military campaigns.

Tolui died (of alcoholism apparently) when Kublai was about fifteen. Kublai's upbringing was always in his mother's hands. She saw that her child learned to ride, to hunt, and to master military technique. His mother had him tutored in reading and writing and the Mongol language. He probably could not read or write Chinese, but could understand and speak the language.

After her husband's death, Kublai's mother got the khan to put the Hebei province of China in her charge. She ruled over Chinese farmers who lived much differently from Mongol pastoral nomads. But instead of imposing the Mongol way of life on the peasants, she encouraged the natives in developing their own economy. By refusing to exploit the Chinese, she was able to draw even greater revenues from flourishing farm communities.

Kublai learned by his mother's example. In 1236, when he was only sixteen, the khan made the youngster lord of a Chinese region with about ten thousand households. Because Kublai operated from Mongolia as an absentee ruler, local officials began to enrich themselves by harsh exploitation of the peasants. Many farmers fled rather than submit to it. When Kublai found out what was going on, he at once introduced new policies, earned the confidence of the peasants, and induced many of the refugees to return home. Prosperity and stability were restored.

One sign of the political wisdom of Kublai's mother is seen in her toleration of all religions. She herself was a Nestorian Christian, but one who did not discriminate against other religions in the Mongol world. She made room for all: Buddhists, Taoists, Muslims. She helped fund their temples, mosques, and schools. One of Kublai's most important advisers was his second wife, Chabi, an ardent Buddhist. He married her when he was about twenty-five, and took two other wives afterward. He had four households, each presided over by a wife, and twelve sons.

young Kublai Khan

Like his grandfather and mother, Kublai sought the help of advisers of what-

The English author Samuel Taylor Coleridge wrote a mysterious poem about Kublai Khan in 1797. It is considered one of the major creations of the romantic period. Coleridge, when he was twenty-five, had been living in a lonely farmhouse. One night he was browsing in the *Pilgrimage*, a collection of folktales published by Samuel Purchas in 1614. In it he was reading the story of how Kubla (as the name was spelled in Coleridge's time) Khan "commanded a palace to be built, and a stately garden thereunto" when he fell into a profound sleep. It was in his sleep, Coleridge said, that he composed the poem. And when he woke, he remembered the lines and eagerly wrote them down. Before he could finish, a person from the nearby village of Porlock called on him and stayed for more than an hour. But when the man was gone, Coleridge could not recall the end of the poem.

Here is what he wrote down:

In Xanadu did Kubla Khan
A stately pleasure-dome decree:
Where Alph, the sacred river, ran
Through caverns measureless to man
    Down to a sunless sea.
So twice five miles of fertile ground
With walls and towers were girdled round:
And there were gardens bright with sinuous rills,
Where blossomed many an incense-bearing tree;
And here were forests ancient as the hills,
Enfolding sunny spots of greenery.

But oh! that deep romantic chasm which slanted
Down the green hill athwart a cedarn cover!
A savage place! as holy and enchanted
As e'er beneath a waning moon was haunted
By woman wailing for her demon-lover!
And from this chasm, with ceaseless turmoil seething,
As if this earth in fast thick pants were breathing,
A mighty fountain momently was forced:

Amid whose swift half-intermitted burst
Huge fragments vaulted like rebounding hail,
Or chaffy grain beneath the thresher's flail:
And 'mid these dancing rocks at once and ever
It flung up momently the sacred river.
Five miles meandering with a mazy motion
Through wood and dale the sacred river ran,
Then reached the caverns measureless to man,
And sank in tumult to a lifeless ocean:
And 'mid this tumult Kubla heard from far
Ancestral voices prophesying war!

      The shadow of the dome of pleasure
      Floated midway on the waves;
      Where was heard the mingled measure
      From the fountain and the caves.
It was a miracle of rare device,
A sunny pleasure-dome with caves of ice!

      A damsel with a dulcimer
      In a vision once I saw:
      It was an Abyssinian maid,
      And on her dulcimer she played,
      Singing of Mount Abora.
Could I revive within me
Her symphony and song,
To such a deep delight 'twould win me,
That with music loud and long,
I would build that dome in air,
That sunny dome! Those caves of ice!
And all who heard should see them there,
And all should cry, Beware! Beware!
His flashing eyes, his floating hair!
Weave a circle round him thrice,
And close your eyes with holy dread,
For he on honey-dew hath fed,
And drunk the milk of Paradise.

Kublai Khan

ever faith. Chinese counselors taught him Confucianism, which stressed the duties of a virtuous ruler. For some years, one of Kublai's most trusted advisers was a Chinese monk, Liu Ping-Chung. He was a man of many talents, a fine painter and calligrapher, a poet, a notable mathematician and astronomer. With other Chinese scholars he devised a new and more precise calendar for the Mongols. He urged Kublai to nurture and protect the scholar-officials as national treasures.

At one time Kublai had some twenty Confucian scholars in his advisory circle. Non-Chinese too were welcomed for their practical help in ruling his domain. He used foreigners not only as advisers but also as scribes, interpreters, tutors, merchants, and even soldiers.

A primary goal of Kublai was uniting all China under his command. That meant conquering the south's Sung dynasty, whose capital was where modern Hangzhou is. But feuding among the Mongols delayed progress for many years. Not until 1278 was the last Sung resistance overcome, ending that dynasty. Now all China was under the dynastic name Kublai took, the Yuan (meaning "Great Originator") dynasty.

In that vast empire the Chinese greatly outnumbered the Mongols. One estimate holds that about three hundred thousand Mongols lived in China. But the Chinese population of the North numbered some ten million, and in the South, about fifty million. So if his reign was to succeed, Kublai realized he must gain the cooperation of the Chinese while preserving the Mongols' own prized cultural heritage.

In so great an empire good communications were vital. Within China Kublai did much to improve the system. To move grain grown in the South to feed hungry mouths in the North, he extended the Grand Canal northward, joining the Yellow River and the Mongol capital. Building it required the labor of two and a half million workers. Along the canal's banks he constructed a stone highway, stretching 1,090 miles.

Kublai improved the famed postal service too. The fourteen hundred postal

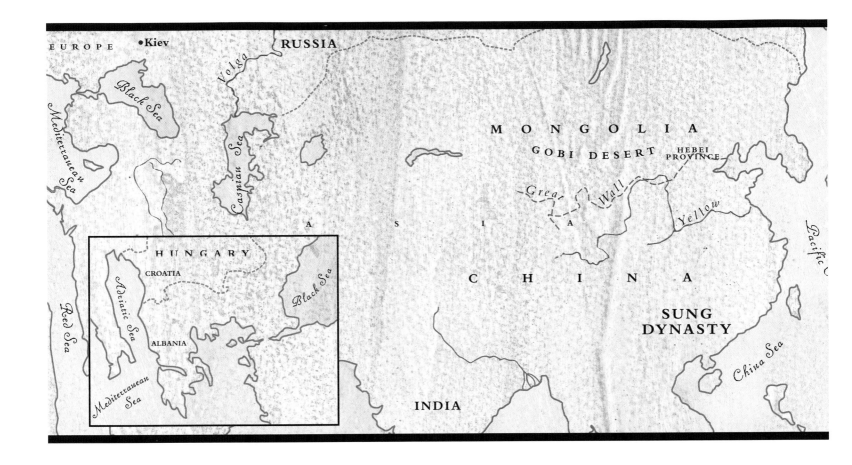

stations were manned by conscripted labor. He placed fifty thousand horses, thousands of oxen and mules, four thousand carts, and six thousand boats in the service. Long before creation of the romanticized efficiency of the pony express of the American West, Kublai had replacements timed to leave stations the moment a postal rider arrived.

To gain more efficiency in government, Kublai simplified and streamlined it. He divided China into six provinces, each with local governing bodies. Agents from the central government oversaw local officials, whether Mongol or Chinese, to ensure that they remained honest. But as with many governments, at all times, bribery and graft were still serious problems.

Kublai also introduced a new legal system, embracing elements of both Mongol and Chinese law. It seems to have been more lenient and flexible than earlier law.

One may wonder why the Chinese were willing to help a conqueror who was not ethnically Chinese. One answer is that the Chinese had long been used to governance by foreigners. Some cooperated with the khan in exchange for money or special privileges. Others hoped Kublai would improve the condition of the Chinese people and perhaps himself become more Chinese in thought and action. But Kublai was no puppet in anyone's hands. He was careful not to become overreliant on foreigners.

With Mongol armies successful in overrunning a vast area of Asia and Europe, Kublai was ready to conquer outlying countries of East Asia. In 1264 he moved the Mongol capital south from Karakorum in the steppe to Beijing in northeast China. He took the title Emperor of China. Architects got busy designing an immense compound for the royal palace and the corps of bureaucrats who would serve the ruler.

The habit of conquest was scarcely interrupted. Kublai had to continue expanding the empire because his own people, the Mongols, measured a ruler's success by his ability to add territory, wealth, and people to his domain. And in the eyes of the Chinese, a great ruler's glory would make other peoples eager to enter Chinese civilization. Kublai sent expeditions into Burma (now Myanmar), Korea, Vietnam, Java, and Japan. Their success was mixed. Japan and Vietnam were failures. The Mongols were superb horsemen but had little experience as sailors. Kublai invaded Japan and was beaten back. Years later he tried again, this time quitting when a great typhoon destroyed his fleet and sailors.

In later life Kublai changed from a strong, healthy, vibrant leader to a grossly fat and sickly old man. Rheumatism and gout plagued him. When his favorite wife, Chabi, died, followed by their son, the heir apparent, he became so depressed that he could hardly function. In 1295 Kublai died. His body was taken to Mongolia and buried. No one knows where the grave is.

Under Kublai's successors—there were seven in the next seventy-four years—Mongol control of China weakened. The empire split into separate states. Finally a popular Chinese uprising drove out the Mongol foreigners.

Though the Mongol empire lasted only about a century, it linked Asia with Europe, beginning a period of fruitful contacts and exchanges between East and West. Under Kublai's policies life in his realm became more peaceful. He never persecuted other religions. He broadened and deepened culture and supported artists, writers, scholars, and scientists.

Historians regard Kublai as one of the great rulers of history. His powerful mind and imagination enabled him to see beyond the nomad mentality of his ancestors and to wisely govern the huge empire of an ancient civilization. Despite persistent tales of "violent Mongol hordes," Kublai's reign demonstrates there was another and brighter side to Mongol history.

Mansa Musa

Humankind began in Africa. From that continent, scientists agree, people slowly moved into other parts of the globe. Analysts of the fossil record, of DNA, and of the relations among human languages agree that it was about one hundred thousand years ago that the ancestors of all modern humans lived in Africa. Around then a small band crossed the isthmus of Suez to begin populating the rest of the globe. By some fifteen thousand years ago there were human beings on every continent but Antarctica.

These earliest groups hunted, fished, and gathered wild fruits and vegetables for food. They learned to make tools and to make fire. About eight thousand years ago they learned how to plant wild seeds and roots to grow their own food. And when farming started, and there was enough food for all, people settled in villages that might grow into towns and cities.

But what about Africa, where it all began? The continent is the second largest on earth; only Asia is bigger. Africa contains 22 percent of the earth's land surface. You could fit the United States, China, India, plus Europe from the Atlantic to Moscow, and much of South America as well, within the African coastline.

Yet most of us who live outside Africa know little about its history and its peoples. It was only about fifty years ago that the veil of ignorance and misunderstanding began to lift. Up to that time it was commonly said that there was no African history to learn; there was only the history of what Europeans did when they came to Africa.

Racism had much to do with that colossal ignorance—racism not as human error, but as a conscious and systematic weapon of exploitation. To declare black people to be inferior, even subhuman, provided a moral justification for enslaving them. The lies of racism made it possible to pretend that black people had no history, no culture worth learning about and learning from.

Basil Davidson, a modern historian of Africa, puts it this way: "A great and growing number of scholars of many nations have accepted that the study of Africa's past is not only possible, but is also useful, and even indispensable, to any understanding of the general condition of humanity, whether in Africa or not."

The history of people on whatever continent they settled varies considerably. "History followed different courses for different people because of differences among peoples' environments, not because of biological differences among peoples themselves." That is the conclusion reached by Jared Diamond in his book *Guns, Germs and Steel*. What Africans did or didn't do depended upon the resources available to them—the plants, animals, and climate. "The climate, disease and a host of other environmental difficulties made Africa a hard place to flourish," the historian K. Anthony Appiah points out.

One of the most famous and powerful kings in African history was Mansa Musa. *(Mansa* means "king.")* He ruled over the empire of Mali in the first part of the fourteenth century. During his reign he extended the empire to its eminence as one of the largest states on the African continent. It embraced a great part of the middle region of West Africa, from beyond the Niger River in the east to the Atlantic Ocean in the west.

The people of Mali belong to one of Africa's several ethnic groups, the Sudanese. But that group itself is a mixture, formed as successive waves of people migrated in and out of the region, in both the remote and the recent past.

What we know about Mansa Musa and his empire comes from the research of many modern scholars. Their writings are based upon a study of medieval sources (chiefly in the Arabic language), on the traditions of oral history, on archaeologic findings, and on the accounts of travelers who visited Mali. Next to Egypt, Mali has the richest deposit of artifacts in Africa.

The oral sources are men called griots, meaning "remembrancers of history." Some have been singers of famous songs and counselors of rulers. They are the human storehouses of the deeds of kings of old, passing from one generation to the next the happenings worth recalling, events that would otherwise vanish. "We are the memory of mankind," as one of them said. "By my mouth you will learn the history of Mali."

All the sources scholars use are valuable. But they are not perfect. A griot's memory may be faulty, or he may romanticize, or twist the facts to suit his own bias. Sometimes sources, oral or written, may contradict one another. A place may be mentioned that has disappeared from the map. Travelers' reports, many written by outsiders, can exaggerate or slip into fantasy. With that caution, do your best to approach the truth.

Even with a wealth of artifacts, not much is known about the ancient history of Mali, when you compare it with other parts of the ancient world. What broke the silence was the arrival of the Muslim Arabs who invaded North Africa in the seventh century and began to use the Sahara as a highway. That desert and the trading across it played a great role in Mali's history.

The Sahara is by far the largest desert in the world, covering 3.5 million square miles, or almost the entire northern third of Africa. From west to east it stretches thirty-two hundred miles. Today it runs through

griot

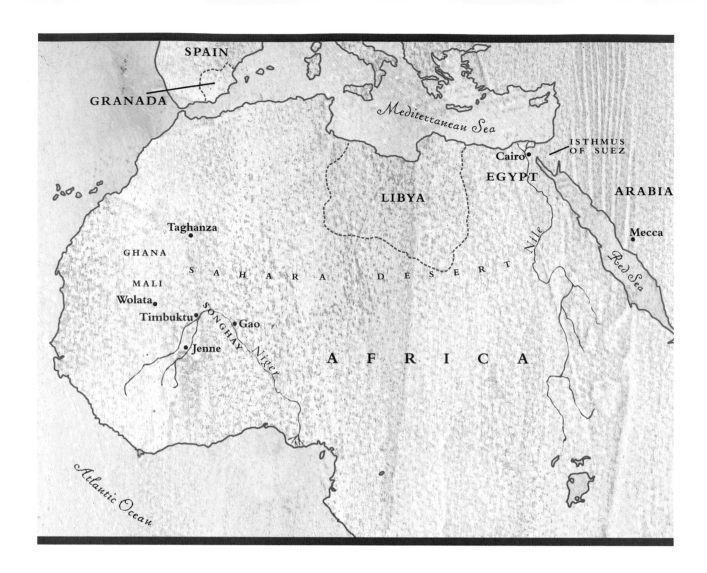

eleven countries and continues to expand, displacing many people and swallowing up villages and towns.

When the Arabs established their control over northern Africa, they gradually converted Africans, especially the upper class—the royal clans, urban people, merchants—to their religion, Islam. The masses kept to their traditional religions. The converts adopted the Arabic language too. It was Islamic travelers who left us detailed accounts of the crossing of the vast desert and of the life they observed in Mali.

What reshaped and energized the trans-Sahara trade was the introduction of the camel by Arabs in the seventh century A.D. Chariots, horses, and donkeys could not do the job nearly as well. The camel was the only animal for the passage over enormously difficult, dry terrain. It could cover great distances across sand with relative ease. It could bear more weight. It could travel for longer periods without water. And if the worst happened, and travelers neared madness and death for lack of water, the camel could be sacrificed to obtain the water stored in its body.

The camel would be the basic means of desert transport for over two millennia—until the modern motor vehicle replaced it. But even with motorized transportation, crossing the desert is no joyride. The Sahara has always been a menace. The distances are so great that anything can happen on the way. The weather can turn terrible; sandstorms can obliterate the world; food and water and fuel can run out. Caravans have been wiped out in the crossing. Survivors report never having been so frightened in their lives.

With Islam's conquest of North Africa, Arabic language and culture spread gradually west across the Sahara. Trade multiplied with the advance of Islam. Old market towns grew bigger, and new ones were created. The trade was carried on by bartering one commodity for another. Some commodities were more in demand and came to be used as currency—gold coins, cowrie shells, strips of cotton cloth, metal ingots.

Traders dealt in farm products, glassware, textiles, pottery, livestock, and animal products, but above all in salt, gold, and slaves. There were salt mines in the desert and gold mines within the empire region. The location of the gold mines was a closely guarded secret, for they were the major source of wealth for the rulers.

The demand for gold was the engine that propelled the growth of states in West Africa. Not because the Africans themselves valued gold that highly. They preferred copper and iron. These were much more useful for weapons and tools. Though there was plenty of gold nearby, the metal had no practical, religious, or even ornamental purpose in sub-Saharan Africa. Until, that is, the demand for gold from the north affected the region, and gold became a vital element of trade.

The Arab traders who brought not only goods but the Muslim religion to West Africa a thousand years ago found societies of small settlements and low population density when they arrived. The most important state at that time was Ghana. The people knew the use of iron and had made both farming tools and weapons of the metal. They could produce more food than their neighbors and, with stronger military power, enlarged their state by conquest. They established a trading system built on the exchange of their gold for salt. They made traders pay high taxes on the buying and selling of gold and salt. To ensure the safety of trade and tax collection, the kings developed a system of justice, of law and order.

Islamic mosque

In the eleventh century A.D., attacks by the Mandingo people of West Africa disrupted Ghana and ended its empire. The Mandingo people built their empire, Mali, on top of Ghana's and created a domain several times larger than that of their predecessor. At its height Mali ran a thousand miles inland, from the Atlantic coast to the border of what is now Nigeria.

Mali was part of the Islamic world, with links strengthened by trade and a shared religion. Several kings in succession ruled it for some seventy-five years until around 1312, when Mansa Musa took the throne. The empire then included rich goldfields, salt mines, and many trading centers. Once an alliance of states governed by chiefs, it was now an empire with dependent provinces, all ruled by the king. (The word *Mali* signifies the place where the king lives.)

During and after Mansa Musa's time, the trans-Sahara trade expanded tremendously. The Arab historian Ibn-Khaldun was told in 1353 that one caravan carrying goods between Egypt and Mali consisted of twelve thousand camels!

Who mined the salt and the gold that were so vital a part of the trade? The major salt mines were in a district called Taghanza. It was a treeless region with poor-quality water and infested with flies. The townsfolk were all slave laborers, wrote the traveler Ibn Battuta, working for their masters, a Berber tribe. They lived on dates, camel meat, and millet. Their houses and even their mosque were made of blocks of salt. While the slaves lived poorly, the salt they mined sold at the market for four or five times the price at the point of production. The salt was used not only as a preservative and an ingredient of food but also as a medium of exchange.

The tribal people who controlled the gold sources were secretive about where the gold mines were and also protective of their personal independence. If any kings of Mali tried to dictate terms to them, they halted production—went on strike, we'd say—or reduced it considerably—the slowdown, a modern union tactic.

Mansa Musa and the kings before him were Muslims from very early on. Ibn Battuta found that Islamic law was applied in Mali. The people studied and memorized the Koran, and the children were raised on it. He also praised Mali's system of law:

> They are seldom unjust, and have a greater abhorrence of injustice than any other people. Their sultan shows no mercy to anyone who is guilty of the least act of it. There is complete security in their country. Neither traveler nor inhabitant in it has anything to fear from robbers or men of violence. They do not confiscate the property of any white man who dies in their country, even if it be uncounted wealth. On the contrary, they give it into the charge of some trustworthy person among the whites, until the rightful heir takes possession of it.

Next to trade, scholarship was the most influential contribution Islam made to Mali. Several towns became major centers of learning. Islamic culture urged the value of literacy so as to be able to read, memorize, and recite the Koran. Religious schools went beyond that to help students master such complex subjects as mathematics, geography, history, logic, the physical sciences, and philosophy. Mali's towns Timbuktu, Jenne, Gao, and Wolata promoted the development of a scholarly tradition. Arabic was the language used by the communi-

In Timbuktu, a famed center of Islamic scholarship in Mansa Musa's time, slavery is still practiced. Its origins in this part of Africa go back to long before Portuguese ship captains began to export black slaves from this region in the 1500s. In precolonial Africa the rate of natural population growth achieved by marriage and begetting was low. In a region where food production was uncertain, a poor family might make a swap with a rich family: a child for a supply of grain. Thus both the child and its parents would have a better chance for survival.

The practice was relatively mild at first, but in time became subject to abuse and to the commercial slave trade. At least eighteen million slaves were exported from tropical Africa between the 1500s and the late 1800s. Across the Atlantic to the Americas went eleven million; another five million across the Sahara or via the Red Sea to North Africa and the Mediterranean lands; and two million more were sent out from East Africa across the Indian Ocean and the South Atlantic to Arabia, India, and China.

When Mali developed close links with the Islamic world, the slave trade became an important part of the relationship. Slavery was known in the Arab region before the advent of Islam. The Islamic religion did not forbid its practice. Although most of the slaves were African, many came from non-African peoples. Despite this fact, Arabic literature reflects negative stereotypes about black Africans.

ty of scholars. Those whose achievements were great might earn power, wealth, and fame. Often they became their region's most notable citizens.

Timbuktu alone was reported to have at least 150 schools, with free tuition offered to promising students. They were taught by a number of scholars; many of these had large collections of books in their personal libraries.

Arabs were not the only ones engaged in the slave trade. Other slavers included Africans, Turks, Persians, Indians, and others. They gathered, sold, bought, transported, and owned slaves.

Slaves were important in almost all aspects of life in Mali: the economy, the military, the civil service. In Mali the great majority of slaves were war captives. The monarchs, like Mansa Musa, were major owners of slaves, who were used as household servants, concubines, entertainers, soldiers, and palace guards.

Today, in some countries of Africa, slavery is still practiced, as human rights groups have reported. Slavery and slave raiding, carried out by armed Arab militias, continue in some countries of Africa. The great majority of the victims are children between the ages of 8 and 14. It was reported that boys were sold for the equivalent of $240 and girls for $160.

The United Nations does what it can in the struggle against slavery and slavelike practices, and the trade in slaves. Its moral authority represents the collective conscience of humanity. But the abolition of the remnants of slavery will occur only through economic development programs that would raise living standards in the poorer nations and thus eliminate the basic cause of slavery.

The kings of Mali crossed the Sahara to visit other Islamic countries. Although royalty in North Africa and Egypt welcomed these possessors of wealth, they seem never to have visited Mali in their turn.

There is a legend holding that the king who preceded Mansa Musa sent a fleet of two hundred ships across the Atlantic Ocean to find out what was at

the far end of it. After a long time, only one ship returned. The captain reported that after sailing on and on, all the ships but his were seized by a powerful
current that carried them away. On hearing that news, the king himself, unable
to believe the story, led an expedition of two thousand ships on a second voy-
age of discovery. But he too, and all his ships and sailors, never returned. And
that is how Mansa Musa was said to have inherited the throne of Mali. The legend has led historians to wonder whether Africans might have crossed the
Atlantic ahead of Christopher Columbus—which could mean that Africans
landed in the Americas before the trans-Atlantic slave trade began.

With his military power, Mansa Musa claimed, he was able to expand the
empire by conquering an additional fourteen provinces and twenty-four cities.
He led the largest army in West Africa: one hundred thousand troops, including ten thousand cavalrymen. The expensive horses they rode were bought
from the Arabs. The soldiers' weapons included bows and arrows, lances,
swords, spears, and maces. So big had Mali grown that it now took four months
to travel from one end to the other.

The longest trip Mansa Musa made was his pilgrimage to Mecca, the holy
city in Arabia. The pilgrimage is one of the most important obligations in Islam.
Believers are expected to perform it at least once in a lifetime. Mansa Musa
began his celebrated journey in 1324 and returned in 1325. The grandeur of his
pilgrimage made Arab writers pay great attention to it. The result was to ele-
vate Mansa Musa's name to the peak of Africa's medieval history.

The two features of his journey most strongly emphasized were the great
size of his entourage and the almost incredible amount of gold that was taken
along, and spent. One writer held that eight thousand people accompanied the
mansa. Another wrote it was twenty thousand, and a third said no, it was sixty
thousand. It is not possible to know the accurate number. One can only say that
there must have been thousands. It is clear that among them were Mansa Musa's
wife, Inari Kunate, other family members, nobles, soldiers, merchants, theolo-
gians, some common folk, and slaves.

The monarch rode on horseback. Preceding him were five hundred slaves, each carrying a staff of pure gold weighing more than five pounds. Bringing up the rear were eighty camels weighted down with gold amounting to two thousand pounds.

It took the king and his people several months to cross the Sahara, passing through Algeria and Libya before they reached Cairo in Egypt. On arrival, the *mansa* sent a rich gift of gold to the sultan. So much gold was spent in Cairo that the value of the precious metal dropped on the market and stayed low for several years.

After a long stay in Cairo (some said it was for a year) the pilgrimage went on to Mecca, a forty-day journey. There Mansa Musa performed all the rites required in the holy city. He generously distributed much gold to pilgrims as well as to the residents of Mecca.

Both trade and commerce flourished during the pilgrimage, for people profited by providing goods and services to the worshipers. Most important, of course, was the religious purpose, but in addition the journey provided the opportunity for pilgrims from all over to meet and get to know other believers. One among these was Es-Saheli, a renowned poet and architect from Granada in Spain. He traveled with Mansa Musa back to Mali, adding to the *mansa*'s renown by designing both the great mosque in Timbuktu and a splendid palace for the king.

Although the pilgrimage proved so costly that Mali incurred heavy debts, it put on display for all the world to see the wealth and power of an African kingdom. Wealth was more a measure of prestige in that time than a means of investment. As one observer said, wealth could buy the loyalty of others, rather than the labor of others. A few years after the journey to Mecca, European cartographers began to create beautiful maps with portraits of Mansa Musa, describing him as the richest and noblest king in West Africa.

In 1337, after a reign of twenty-five years, Mansa Musa died. His empire gradually declined, and part of it was taken over by the rising empire of Songhay.

Atahualpa

Reigned A.D. circa 1525-1533

Atahualpa was a king whose name is probably less familiar to you than any of the other rulers in this book. He was the Inca emperor who was captured and murdered by Francisco Pizarro in 1533.

Pizarro and the other Spanish conquistadores were among the European adventurers who seized vast lands in the Americas after the landing of Columbus. The Spanish settlers were hungry for land, for gold, and for glory. They were a poor, tough, and ambitious lot out for booty, though they talked constantly of carrying the message of Jesus to the benighted heathens of the New World.

The age of the conquistadores began in 1513, when Balboa crossed the Isthmus of Panama and became the first European to see the Pacific. Then came Hernán Cortés. In 1519 he landed on the coast of Mexico and began the march inland that ended in the conquest of the Aztec Empire. A dozen years later Pizarro launched an expedition to Peru, the land of the Incas.

Wherever they went in opening up new chapters in the history of imperialism, the Spaniards had superior armaments. This superiority lay not so much in their guns, for in those times guns were hard to load and fire, and Pizarro had only a dozen of them. Far more important were their steel swords, lances, and daggers. The Incas fought with slings (to hurl egg-size stones), javelins, bolas (thrown to entangle an enemy's legs), spiked maces, and war clubs with star-shaped heads. But such weapons were not very effective against steel armor and steel helmets.

The greatest advantage was given by the Spaniards' horses, animals unknown in the Americas of that day. Their use of cavalry accounts for the way Spaniards so often won battles against enormous odds. The shock of a cavalry charge and the speed of such attacks left foot soldiers almost helpless.

As the Spanish moved south of Mexico, they encountered people of many different cultures. But none would be so extraordinary as the most distant: the Andean civilization of the Inca Empire, whose ruler was Atahualpa.

The Incas called their empire Tahuantinsuyu, "Land of the Four Quarters." At that time it was the biggest native state in the western hemisphere. By armed conquest the masters of this empire had taken over the Andes, the most rugged mountain chain on earth except for the even higher Himalayas in Asia. Inca armies had ranged far beyond their capital at Cuzco in Peru to dominate many tribes and their varied societies. The empire of Atahualpa extended from the edge of the Amazon rain forest in the east to the Pacific Ocean in the west. At its height, the empire's area was 380,000 square miles. It included large parts of what are today the countries of Ecuador, Bolivia, Peru, Argentina, and Chile. No Andean country of today equals it in size or prosperity.

Stretching down the mountainous Andean backbone of South America was a great variety of plants, animals, and people. Tribes of both large and small populations lived in the Andes region, each with its own ethnic identity and a powerful desire to remain independent. How could anyone build an empire out of such conflicting elements? To conquer small ethnic groups was relatively easy. But then to unite them into a national whole? The Incas succeeded in doing this, at least for a time.

But before describing how the Incas did it, let's look at their name. It is the term for a small group of kinfolk, perhaps forty thousand, who built the Inca state by force of arms. They were the empire's governing nobility. The head of this ruling group was the Supreme Inca. At the empire's peak about ten million people were his subjects. *They* were not Incas, however, for that was a closed ethnic group.

Where did the Incas come from? The Americas were colonized, historians agree, by a few small groups of people who crossed the Bering land bridge from Siberia into Alaska and gradually moved down into strange territory. This happened fourteen thousand or more years ago. Some of these people eventually reached Central America and crossed the Isthmus of Panama to enter South America.

The Andean landscape is rich in environmental extremes—high altitude, desert, and tropics. So as the early arrivals dispersed, they developed ways to make their living with whatever resources nature provided. Their ingenuity and adaptability enabled them to build viable communities in mountain, coastal, desert, or jungle habitats.

It never was easy. As the archaeologist Michael Moseley puts it, "Andean landscapes subject people to stress from a variety of sources. For the majority, who traditionally resided above . . . 10,000 feet, the corollaries of high altitude include elevated solar radiation, cold, high winds, rough terrain, limited farm land, poor soils, aridity, erratic rainfall, short growing seasons, diminished nutrition, and hypoxia. . . . Earthquakes occur every generation or so, triggering hundreds of mountain avalanches, reshaping the landscape and killing thousands of people. Major volcanic eruptions are less frequent but they too alter landscapes."

Although archaeologists have unearthed a great deal of information about the pre-Columbian Andean world, how the Inca civilization got started is still uncertain. Legends handed down orally give us some idea, however undocumented. The ancestors of the Incas were said to be born of the sun god and

terraced farms

were sent to Cuzco to found a new culture. Stories are told about at least a dozen Inca emperors, the last of them Atahualpa. It is not until the ascent of the ninth emperor, Pachacutec, that dates and events can be linked to historical evidence.

For untold centuries the Incas were only one of many ethnic groups living in the valleys around what would later become the city of Cuzco. The Andes region contained many such small, warring tribes. Inca leaders began to play them off against one another and thus conquered them piece by piece. As the Incas consolidated such areas, they went on to conquer neighboring lands.

Recent research suggests that the Inca dynasty began around A.D. 1200. By 1400 the Incas had developed a true state. But they were not without rivals. They competed for power with others, especially with the Chanco people, who had also formed a strong confederacy. A fierce battle between the rival states took place, perhaps around 1438, with the Incas victorious. That victory won Pachacutec the throne and the title of Inca.

He chose Cuzco to be his capital and led his army from there in a series of expeditions to increase his power and expand the Inca borders. Sometimes the troops had to return to old places to put down revolts by subjugated peoples opposed to Inca rule.

Running what had become a huge empire that included many ethnic groups speaking various languages and practicing local customs was a constant challenge. How did the Inca rulers manage it?

First, let's look at the base of any community's life: the way people make a living. The Inca economy was rooted in agriculture. The chief crops were the potato, corn (maize), quinoa (a plant with grainlike seeds), beans, squash, and peppers. More than two hundred varieties of the potato were grown in Inca lands. *Chuño*—freeze-dried potato—is still one of the most widely used foods in the Andes. There was fishing in river, lake, and sea, and herding of animals such as the llama and the alpaca. The llama served mainly as a pack animal, while the alpaca was bred for its wool. Both animals provided manure for fertilizer and, occasionally, meat, leather, and bone.

Coca too was grown, a special plant of "magical" powers. Coca had a role in the Inca religion and was frequently scattered or burned as an offering to the gods. When leaves of the plant were chewed and mixed with lime or potash, narcotic substances were released that suppressed hunger, thirst, and fatigue.

This was no system of private enterprise. Nor was the government in any sense democratic. Rather you could call it a totalitarian society: rigid governmental control over a highly organized form of production and distribution was exercised by a power at the top. At the bottom was the basic economic unit—the married couple, family, or household. It was not self-sufficient. Farming and herding under the difficult conditions of the Andean world required cooperative effort in carrying out several tasks at one time, and often in different places. In the Andes a collective based on kinship developed, called the *ayllu*. It was a group of related people who exchanged labor and engaged in cooperative management of land and herds.

As a member of the *ayllu* you had the responsibility to help others and a claim upon them to help you. In considering marriage, your best choice might be a partner with the most relatives—to share work, resources, and benefits.

Still, the Andean system did not bring about full equality. Some people inherited, or married into a group with, far more resources than others. So there were rich couples and rich families, and a lot of quite poor people. No matter how far back in time you go, it seems, always, that some people were better off than others.

Ayllus were governed by hereditary rulers. They were viewed as intermediaries between heaven and earth. They were praised when things went well and blamed when they went badly. They mediated quarrels and saw to it that each household had field and pasture enough to meet their needs. While these leaders supervised everything, the *ayllus* in return supplied all their needs.

A small number of people, perhaps 10 percent of the total population, held the highest posts in local and national government. An upper level made the most important decisions while a lower level saw that the decisions were carried out. At the peak of power was the royal family of Cuzco, the "true Incas." A level below was a class of people recruited generally from the nobility or leadership of peoples conquered by the Incas. They held the title of Inca by appointment and honor, not by ancestry.

There was another sizable class of people who were subsidized because of occupations that required highly trained skills. These included accountants, surveyors, engineers, and hydrologists. Skilled artisans and craftspeople—potters, weavers, metallurgists, jewelers—were also supported by the state. The most highly skilled specialists were taken from subject provinces and resettled in the Cuzco area to serve the needs of royalty, nobility, and religion.

Pachacutec, inspired by the sun god, was credited with inventing the governmental structure. The empire's taxation system, its highway and communication systems, and its extensive warehousing system were all his work, it is believed.

Ordinary people did not own land. It belonged to the *ayllu*. The yield of a third of the land in an *ayllu* was set aside for the empire's gods and the local priests and shrine attendants. Another third went to the emperor, the royal court, and the military. The last third was for the local community, and reallocated yearly to village members by the local leader. Each family got a share in proportion to its size; when a household grew or shrank, its share changed.

Agricultural taxes were paid by the labor of both men and women. There was also a tax in the form of service asked only of males. Called *mit'a*, it was intended for work on construction projects, service in military campaigns, and the like. With millions of males to draw upon, the Inca Empire was able to handle large projects: a magnificent network of roads, huge irrigation and terracing systems, immense architectural monuments. The building of just one fort in Cuzco was said to take the labor of thirty thousand men at one time. *Mit'a* labor also reclaimed unfarmed land. Wherever necessary in the empire, colonies of *mit'a* workers built multitudes of masonry terraces, like those surrounding Cuzco, to add much-needed farmable land. The state acquired so much surplus agricultural revenue that it built warehouses everywhere to store the food. It should be noted that all this construction work was done without the benefit of the wheel or of pulleys.

Food and beverages were what the ordinary folk received for their work; the top ranks expected more. Their reward usually came in textiles. The Andean

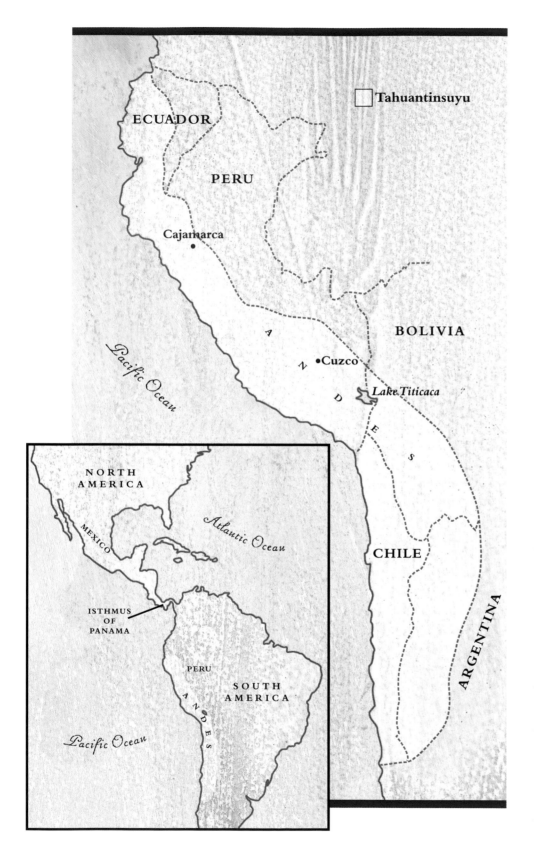

people took pride in dressing their families well, and cloth making, performed by the women, was an important and flourishing craft. Even queens and empresses wove. The high quality of your clothing indicated your rank and status. The heads of state, of course, wore the finest garments. These were rich in color and design and made from such superior fibers as vicuña wool, decorated with gold or silver thread or the brilliant feathers of tropical birds.

Barter was the most common form of exchange. Everything produced, from food to textiles to the fine arts, carried out the functions that money serves today.

Scholars argue about the position of women in the empire. Some believe that women had equal status and that they carried out the same tasks as the men, in field or pasture, and in such crafts as weaving. Pregnant women were relieved of work only in the last few weeks. Usually a mother gave birth alone and then purified herself and the baby in a nearby stream. Family and friends celebrated a birth with presents. When boys reached fourteen, the event was marked with a public ceremony. The puberty of girls was celebrated at home, with family and friends.

There was no public education system. Children of the poor learned the skills of farming and the crafts from their parents, while the elite went to schools exclusively for them. As a member of the royal family, Atahualpa was tutored by uncles or cousins. Boys of high rank attended a four-year course of study that included the spoken language of the Inca, theology, geography, arithmetic, astronomy, and the use of the quipu. The quipu was a cluster of knotted strings used for calculating and for recording statistics and possibly historical events. The colored cords and knots served to touch off chains of memory in the minds of skilled clerks. No people of the Inca Empire, so far as we know, ever had an alphabetic or pictorial system of writing.

Busy as they were, extracting a living from so difficult an environment, the Andes people had time for fun. At their seasonal festivals and religious ceremonies, they danced and sang. Each province of the empire enjoyed its own traditional dances. Flutes and drums provided the music. During festivals people listened to stories and epic poems that had been passed on from generation to generation. Although they had no writing, they had an oral literature that included dramas.

All this began to change, and rapidly, when the civilization of the Old World collided with the civilization of the New World. For millennia the two had developed in complete isolation from each other—until 1492, when Columbus "discovered" Caribbean islands thickly populated with Native Americans.

Forty years later, on November 16, 1532, came the first encounter between Atahualpa, the Inca emperor, and the Spanish conquistador Francisco Pizarro. Each represented a mighty state. Atahualpa was absolute monarch of the biggest and most advanced state of the New World, and Pizarro was the emissary of

Charles V, Holy Roman Emperor and king of Spain, the most powerful state in Europe.

The effects of their meeting, both immediate and long-term, could never have been foreseen. There, at the Peruvian highland town of Cajamarca, stood Pizarro, an illiterate adventurer, with his army of 168 Spaniards. They were one thousand miles south of the nearest Spaniards, in Panama; they were on strange ground; they knew little about the local people and about the emperor they were facing.

But what Pizarro did know was the strategy Cortés used to conquer Montezuma and his Aztec Empire in Mexico. Montezuma had mistakenly taken Cortés for a returning god and had let him and his small army into the Aztec capital of Tenochtitlán. Cortés had then seized Montezuma and gone on to take over his empire.

Opposite Pizarro stood Atahualpa. He knew where he was: in the heart of his own empire of millions of subjects, and around him his army of eighty thousand soldiers, exhilarated by their recent victory in a civil war with other Indians. But Atahualpa knew almost nothing about the Spaniards, their military power, and their goals. True, the Spanish had already conquered most of Central America's Indian societies, but Atahualpa was totally ignorant of this. Nor did he understand that Pizarro represented a power grimly set on permanent conquest, rather than an isolated raid.

Who would you bet on in this conflict between the Spaniard and the Inca?

Within minutes of their meeting, Pizarro captured Atahualpa. And what followed, within an incredibly short time, was the downfall of the Inca Empire.

We know what happened from that day on, for it was written down by six of Pizarro's company and published later on.

Atahualpa was at Cajamarca, relaxing in its warm springs after winning a civil war that had divided and weakened the Incas. The civil war had broken out after a devastating smallpox epidemic, carried into South America by the Spanish, had spread swiftly among the Indians, who lacked any immunity to the

European disease. It reached into the Inca Empire and killed the emperor, his heir, and much of the Inca population. The heir's death led to a battle for the throne between two of the emperor's other sons, Atahualpa and Huascar. Just before Pizarro's arrival, Atahualpa had captured Huascar and imprisoned him at Cuzco.

Pizarro faced an emperor whose power, he knew, had been crippled by both an epidemic and a civil war. Pizarro had also learned, on his march toward Cajamarca, that the people were grumbling against the emperor because of increasingly heavy taxation. If he made the right moves, maybe he could encourage the people to revolt against Atahualpa.

llama

As they met in the city's main square, Atahualpa welcomed Pizarro "as a friend and a brother" and offered him a drink from a great goblet of gold. (Pizarro had concealed his soldiers in various parts of the city nearby.) Pizarro then had a priest approach the emperor and ask him "to subject himself to the law of our lord Jesus Christ and to the service of His Majesty the King of Spain" offering him a Bible and a cross. When the furious Atahualpa threw the Bible down, Pizarro gave the signal for his troops to fire cannon, and both cavalry and infantry rushed out of their hiding places to plunge into the mass of unarmed Indians crowding the square. It was wholesale slaughter, with six or seven thousand Indians killed and many more wounded and captured. Atahualpa himself was taken prisoner. A historian has called this "one of the most atrocious acts of bloodthirsty treachery in recorded history."

Pizarro kept Atahualpa prisoner for eight months while gathering history's largest ransom in return for a promise to free the emperor. The ransom was enough gold to fill a palace room twenty-two feet long by seventeen feet high to a width of over eight feet. When Indians from all over the empire had brought in an enormous number of objects of gold and silver, Pizarro betrayed his promise and killed Atahualpa by strangling him.

The Spaniards had Indian goldsmiths melt down the treasure into ingots of standard size so that the gold could be divided and transported. The total weight came to 13,265 pounds of gold and 26,000 pounds of silver. The value by today's standards was probably about fifty million dollars. The value in lost art objects is beyond measure.

The execution of the emperor was the decisive turn for the Spanish conquest of the Inca Empire. With the empire leaderless, Pizarro placed a brother of Atahualpa on the throne as a puppet ruler while he moved on to plunder the wealth of the capital and other cities. Violent quarrels broke out in his own ranks over the division of the loot. Pizarro, brilliant as a military adventurer, proved totally incompetent as a ruler. He could not control his own people or provide good government for the conquered Incas. In 1541 Pizarro himself was assassinated by Spanish conspirators. The last Inca leader to struggle against the invaders was Tupac Amaru. He was captured and beheaded in 1572.

Why did resistance to the Spaniards fail so badly? Imagine a highly centralized government abruptly losing a leader considered sacred. How could the gods let that happen? The shock threw everything into chaos. The Inca bureaucracy was so rigid that it could not act on its own, without orders from the top, in a crisis. The provinces conquered by the Incas had always chafed under domination; now they would revolt, and even join the Spaniards against a common enemy. Then there were, as always, people unwilling to accept life's injustices; they may have thought things would be better under the new regime. But above all else, the Europeans were so ferocious, so brutal, so inhuman in their rule, so beyond anything the Indians had ever experienced, that not only the Incas but many other civilizations crumbled under such unbearable pressure.

Louis XIV

Reigned A.D. 1643–1715

Louis the fourteenth?

Who were all the other rulers named Louis? They were kings in a long line of monarchs that they traced back to Charlemagne. But the two who wrote blazing pages in history were the fourteenth and the sixteenth—Louis XVI because he was the last in the line, the one overthrown by the French Revolution and executed in 1793. Louis XIV is renowned because he reigned for seventy-two years during a time historians consider the peak of France's glory. Louis lived into old age, dying in 1715. His reign was the longest in European history. He built France into Europe's most powerful nation and made himself the supreme symbol of his age.

Louis XIV, born in 1638, was only one quarter French. He was half Spanish by his mother and a quarter Italian by his grandmother. The mixed origin was not uncommon. Most royal marriages were made not for love but to add power or lands to a throne.

Louis was the son of Louis XIII. When his father died in 1643, Louis was only five. His mother, as regent for the child, took royal authority, but the real power was wielded by her adviser Cardinal Mazarin. He had many successes in diplomacy and war. He built up the power of the monarchy against the nobility, while adding much wealth to his own treasury. But he proved unpopular with almost everyone: the peasants, because they hated the heavy taxes laid on them to pay for war; the merchants, because his policy hurt trade; the nobles, because he saw no virtue in feudalism; local government, because he placed himself and the king above their laws.

Mazarin's enemies tried twice to get rid of him. Both revolts failed, but Mazarin was forced to leave the country. Then in September 1651 Louis, now thirteen, announced he was ending the regency of his mother and taking power into his own hands.

The young and handsome king felt secure enough to welcome Cardinal Mazarin back. Louis knew how brilliant the cardinal was and was ready to learn from him. Treaties were signed with England and Spain that made France the dominant power in Europe. Mazarin saw how capable young Louis was and advised him to be his own chief minister and not to trust major decisions to any others. When the cardinal died in 1661, a secret hiding place was discovered where he had placed his enormous wealth. Louis promptly moved it into his own treasury, making himself the richest monarch of his time.

For a youngster to take decisive charge of a kingdom and go on to expand his power could not have been predicted. The boy's education was limited. While his mother and Mazarin had struggled to maintain power, the child had been neglected. He did little reading in history and knew few facts about it. His mother did have him trained in Catholic doctrine and insisted he learn good manners. "Cherish a sense of honor above all," she said.

Yet Louis had a great will to exercise power. When Mazarin died, the heads of government departments asked Louis, "Where shall we go now to get our instructions?" "To me," he replied. And from that day on he ruled France.

The French were delighted with so handsome a king. At maturity he was only five feet five inches, but the way he carried himself made everyone think he was taller. He was physically strong, a good rider and dancer, skillful at tournament jousting, and a fine storyteller. "His mind," one historian said, was "not as good as his manners." "He had nothing more than good sense," said another, "but he had a great deal of it." As vain as a stage star, he played to the hilt the role of the Sun King, as he was called.

His chief virtue, he himself said, was his love of glory. He preferred a lofty reputation to life itself, he said. And that, as he grew older, proved to be his nemesis.

Louis married Marie-Therese, daughter of the king of Spain. She bore six children, five of them dying in infancy. He was able to turn many a woman's head, both before marriage and after, and had many love affairs. He regarded women only as ornaments—charming, inferior creatures. He liked to see them covered with diamonds.

Louis seriously believed that God had chosen him to govern France. In the Bible he found passages that upheld the divine right of kings. Later in life, to guide his son and heir, he wrote that "God appoints kings the sole guardians of the public weal; they are God's vicars here below." He believed that, to carry out divine authority, kings need unlimited power. Perhaps partly because France had gone through periods of dreadful chaos, people welcomed centralizing power. They hoped it would bring them order, security, and peace.

We link Louis to the legendary magnificence of his court at Versailles. Out of sight is the suffering of the vast mass of the people of France, upon whose backs the superstructure rested. They were at the bottom of the social system.

There were three traditional estates, or classes, in France: those who prayed, those who fought, and those who toiled. The first group embraced the clergy. The second was the nobility. And the third included just about everyone else, but especially the great mass of the peasantry, plus officials, tradespeople, artisans, and urban workers. It was the peasants whose productive labor enabled the other estates of the realm to live and prosper.

France was technologically backward. It had great natural resources, but they were little developed. The Netherlands, not France, was Europe's dominant economic power. France's wealth lay in its fertile land and large and vital

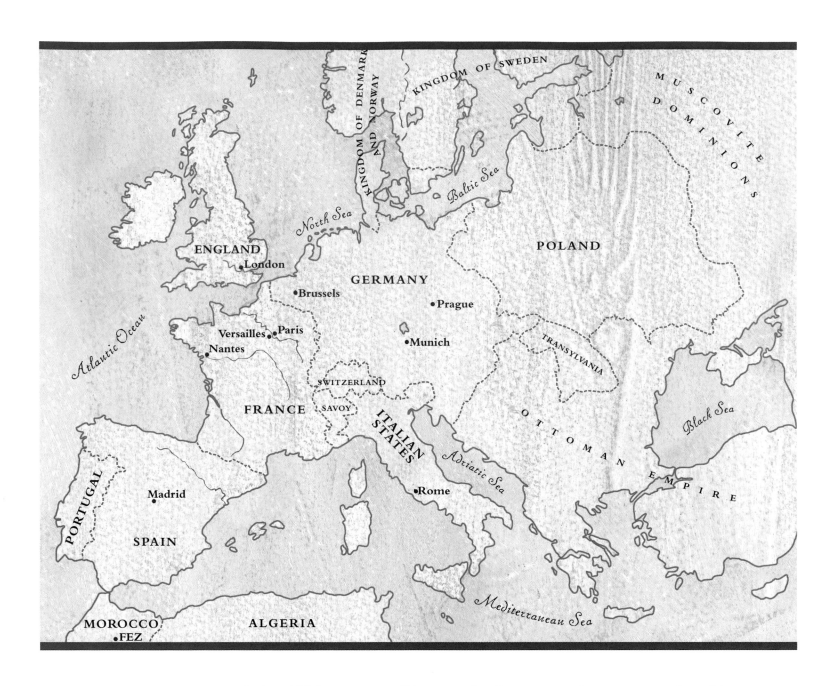

population. With twenty million people, France was the most populous king-dom in Europe. About fifteen million were peasants, and some three million, workers.

The French peasant was a jack-of-all-trades, wrote Pierre Goubert—"mar-ket gardener, mixed farmer, vine-grower, day laborer, spinner or weaver, cloth-worker or blacksmith, nailsmith or innkeeper." And usually poacher or smuggler. Nine out of ten of the king's subjects labored with their hands to allow the other tenth to live in ease.

Members of the nobility—about a hundred thousand families—ate up the revenues from the peasants' labors on the land. How? Through rents, taxes, tithes, and dues of one kind or another. In addition they profited by the pensions and gifts that the king handed out to his most loyal nobles.

Then there was the bourgeoisie, or middle class: officials, state pensioners, people with private incomes, traders, manufacturers. Like the nobles, they owned land, often managing it more profitably than the nobles. Many supervised estates that were owned by Church or nobility, positions that brought in still more income.

It was members of the nobility and the bourgeoisie who staffed the various positions in the Church. The younger sons, who did not inherit family property, filled bishoprics and the best religious institutions and lived off the revenues and dues attached to their offices. Both town and country priests enjoyed a fairly comfortable living.

The geography of France is so varied that every region, province, and town has its own distinct character. Unity of such a country would be hard to create and to maintain. As the historian Fernand Braudel put it, "We are faced with a hundred, a thousand different Frances of long ago, yesterday or today." A jokester spoke of France as "one and *divisible.*" It was like a huge jigsaw puzzle, with each inhabitant personally attached to some little piece of it.

A king who sought to unify this patchwork had to dominate it, to blur its differences, to grab the spotlight for himself, to stamp out any competing powers. A great obstacle to achieving this goal was distance. But distance is not invariable—a mile is not just a mile. Its true measure is the speed at which people can travel it. And in Louis's time people moved slowly! Endless journeys on horseback, in carriages, in stagecoaches along impossible roads. No motor vehicles, no railroads, no airplanes. Nor were there telegraphs, telephones, or E-mail to secure instant communication. It would be an immensely difficult task for Louis to build France into Europe's most powerful nation and to supervise and control it.

But there were other differences in France as well. Not only physical, but cultural, religious, political, and social. Inevitably these meant misunderstanding, suspicion, hostility, and conflict.

Louis felt that his people longed for order and strong government after all the foreign and domestic conflicts they had endured. As the pupil of Mazarin he knew what was needed to increase the instruments of power. From Mazarin's service he took Jean-Baptiste Colbert, a young economist, to help plan the transformation of France. Louis and Colbert wanted to move the country from peasant changelessness and feudal fragmentation to a nationally unified system of agriculture, industry, and finance.

Colbert took on one big job after another, from reorganizing finances to supervising building construction, royal manufactures, commerce, the fine arts, the navy, and even the king's household. He worked harder than anyone else and achieved more than anyone else. Regardless of justice or equity he did whatever he thought was needed to gain the king's goals, not stopping at bribing, imprisoning, or hanging people who stood in his way, including the nobility and the wealthy.

His reforms did least for agriculture. There was no year without a famine somewhere in France, and the king did little about it. In some districts a third of the population died of starvation. In the king's desire to expand industry, Colbert sacrificed agriculture. He kept the price of farm products low so that he could cheaply feed the rising population of the towns and the swelling armies of the king.

Louis and Colbert focused on industry. They brought enterprise under state control, with the government regulating prices, wages, and sales. The high quality standards Colbert established won French products newer and bigger markets abroad. He nationalized the Gobelin tapestry factory, making it world famous for its superb quality.

Louis encouraged or provided scientific and technical education. French workshops became schools for apprentices. An encyclopedia of arts and crafts was published, as were treatises on machines and the mechanical arts. Louis's policy was to put every able-bodied male to work. Orphans were drafted from asylums into industry. Beggars were removed from the streets and placed in factories. But labor had no protection from abuse. Hours were terribly long, wages terribly low. The business class grew richer and the state's income from taxes grew bigger, while the condition of peasants and workers sank to the bottom.

But the king could not have cared less about the poor. Unlike others who protested about the horrible lives of the galley slaves, Louis only increased their numbers and let Colbert commit any injustice to get the slaves required for the galleys. Nor did Louis heed complaints about the filthy dungeons in which prisoners were kept. It seemed that no amount of suffering inflicted on others could move him. "The spirit of Christianity," wrote his biographer Nancy Mitford, "was a closed book to him."

Colbert created royal highways, mostly for military use, which also helped commerce grow. Land travel was always slow, so canals were dug to speed maritime transport. The French navy expanded, and men were forced into its service. French trading companies reached into the West Indies, the East Indies, the Levant, and the northern seas.

This was the time when France expanded its power by founding colonies overseas. Explorers were sent out into several parts of the world, and colonists followed to give France footholds in Canada, West Africa, the Indies, the valleys of the Saint Lawrence and Mississippi Rivers.

Colbert enforced so many regulations that it made him a nuisance. But for a time France enjoyed prosperity under Louis. With Colbert he created the economic form of a modern France.

The king found, however, that in building a unified France he had to make many compromises. Not all the differences among the provinces could be smoothed out. Rather the crown had to adapt itself to them to attain its vital ends. These goals were public order, respect for royal justice, a reliable supply of grain, and the establishment of a tax system. The key tool was the creation of thirty superintendents or administrators to control the provinces. They were loyal servants of the national state with almost unlimited powers.

Louis had a genius for what we call public relations. He made himself the

gardens of Versailles

object of a cult. He wanted the people of France to see him as the best, the greatest, the purest, the "Most Christian King" of a Catholic nation. He calculated his every move to amaze not only the French but all of Europe. He aspired for all to see him as the premiere monarch—number one.

This is why he built Versailles, within easy carriage distance from Paris, and made it his capital. Until then the court was nomadic, moving from one château to another with an army of courtiers, diplomats, and attendants. Sometimes Louis stayed in the old palace in Paris, the Louvre. But it became his strong belief that one path to attaining glory was the creation of magnificent buildings. Colbert took on the job, creating an unrivaled team of experts—engineers, architects, landscape designers, sculptors, and painters.

Together they turned Versailles from an old hunting lodge into an enormous and sumptuous palace with a grand park and pleasure gardens. In 1671, though it was nowhere near finished, the king moved into it, and the neighboring hamlet was transformed into a royal town. At one time there were thirty-six thousand men and six thousand horses working on the enterprise, often in day and night shifts. About six hundred persons made up Louis's court—the royal family, the higher nobility, foreign envoys, and servants. At its peak Versailles's population grew to ten thousand, including many of the great nobles of the realm, some of them temporary guests there to dine, to entertain, to gamble, to receive rewards—or just to be seen. Famous men and beautiful and brilliant women were drawn to Versailles by the promise of money, reputation, and power. The king set the fashion for elaborate ceremony and extravagant dress. Huge sums went into clothing, carriages, servants, and horses. The chief recreation was gambling for high stakes, with millions of francs lost in a night's play. Versailles, to many, seemed heaven on earth.

Were grand palaces enough for Louis's glorification? No; learning from the experience of the great Roman emperor Augustus and Greece in the time of Pericles, Louis too would glorify his person and his reign by bringing the arts and sciences together. He became their great patron. Royal taste did much to shape the cultural life of his age. He set up academies in the arts and sciences under the control of his favorites. Playwrights, musicians, architects, painters, sculptors—whatever their field, they were all linked to an artistic dictatorship, where harmony and order were the governing motives.

Yet it turned out that even Louis had no monopoly over creativity. Yes, there were rules to be followed, but they were not necessarily observed by everyone, or all the time. Many talents flowered under generous patronage and their achievements will always be honored. To name but a few: Molière, Racine, La Fontaine, Boileau, Le Brun, Lully, La Rochefoucauld, and Bossuet.

The aristocracies of Europe applauded French art. Its influence spread to the ruling class in many courts. They looked to Versailles as their model in manners and the arts. Louis could boast of his cultural conquest. He loved art and owned more than two thousand paintings, many by the greatest artists. Music too: he always had a band or orchestra playing nearby.

It was Louis's firm belief that everyone must serve the king. The one being he was willing to serve was God. But that didn't mean the pope. Louis believed that the clergy of his kingdom were *his* servants, and the Church's possessions *his* to dispose of as he liked. Brought up as a Catholic, he knew his task was to defend the faith against all others. He took up the cause of Catholic minorities in Protestant countries. But to Christian minorities in his own country— Huguenots, Jansenists, and Waldensians—he gave no quarter. He regretted that a great many of his own subjects adhered to "the so-called reform religion."

France in the 1590s had been torn by the Wars of Religion. To restore internal peace in 1598, Louis's grandfather, King Henry IV, issued the Edict of Nantes. It defined the rights of Protestants, giving them a virtual state within the state. But both Cardinal Mazarin and Louis himself believed that the edict ran counter to their drive to unify France.

More and more Louis tried to impose uniformity in religious affairs. In the 1680s he intensified persecution of Protestants; his actions made the edict nothing but a scrap of paper. Finally in 1685 he declared that the majority of French Protestants had been converted to Catholicism and that therefore there was no need for the edict. It was revoked.

Now Louis launched a reign of terror. He refused to allow French Protestants to leave the country. He promised that those who remained could worship privately, free of persecution, but never kept the promise. Their churches were torn down, their gatherings forbidden, their children made to attend mass. The Waldensians in Savoy were massacred, and six hundred

Protestants "caught making assemblies" were executed. Perhaps two hundred and fifty thousand fled abroad to escape persecution.

One effect of Louis's intolerance was to weaken the French economy, for many of the Protestants were highly skilled and needed in industry, and others were merchants, bankers, ship-builders, lawyers, and doc-tors. The Protestant nations of England and Germany disliked Louis all the more for his brutality. Louis meant to make France a Catholic state; he only succeeded in driving Protestants under-ground, where they secretly observed their faith. For France it was a great loss of population, wealth, talent, power, and intellect.

Molière

In an age of absolute monarchy, war was "the trade of kings." The military system was based on strict discipline, a centralized administration, the long-term service of highly trained troops. The strong, central economy that Colbert created supplied the king's need for money simply by increasing taxation. The effect on France was great, for the steady run of wars created a demand for manpower. Warfare was no longer the concern of only the upper classes. The cavalry, once the preserve of aristocrats, opened to anyone who could ride a horse. Mercenary regiments drew heavily on the poor of any country. Science and technology were mustered too, especially for the artillery and engineering corps.

The size of armies shot way up in the seventeenth century. Louis XIV kept a military of four hundred thousand men, and in combat fielded armies of one hundred thousand. During his reign the French army emerged as Europe's dominant land force. Whatever the conflict, internal or external, Louis relied on the army as his principal instrument of power.

Louis's power and prestige abroad were bolstered by his foreign policy. He personally ran the most complete diplomatic service Europe had ever known. And he kept his strong military forces ready, to be unleashed only when they were well prepared for war. That didn't guarantee success. Fear of France led European powers to form a coalition against him. His attack on the Holy Roman Empire in 1688, after nine years of inconclusive combat, ended in a treaty that cost him some minor territories. His last war, the lengthy War of the Spanish Succession (1701–1714), left France in debt and greatly weakened militarily.

What about Louis's reputation, the "glory" he sought in war? When his armies destroyed homes and villages by fire and sword, the victims called him a monster, a barbarian, a "Hun dead to all human feelings." In one battle near Brussels in 1693, the slaughter was immense: twenty thousand of the enemy killed and eight thousand of the French.

The French at home acclaimed their generals and their heroic soldiers. The people, however, were exhausted in body and spirit. The drain upon them became unbearable. Revolts broke out in parts of France, and it took the army to restore order. Poverty, famine, disease, and war reduced the population from twenty-three million in 1670 to nineteen million in 1700.

How can the impact of Louis's absolute monarchy be summed up? The historian Barbara Tuchman put it this way: "When Louis XIV, outliving son and grandson, died in 1715 after a reign of 72 years, he bequeathed, not the national unity that had been his objective, but an enlivened and embittered dissent, not national aggrandizement in wealth and power, but a weakened, disordered and impoverished state. He propelled France toward the collapse that could only result, as it did two reigns later, in the overturn of absolute monarchy."

Peter the Great

Measure him by almost any standard and Peter the Great comes out a giant. The Russian czar's life is an example of the power of a great personality to change his people and his world.

To start with, Peter Alekseevich Romanov was big—six feet, seven inches tall. Not so impressive in our time, when many athletes soar even higher, but three hundred years ago Peter towered over almost everyone. And then there was his giant ego. From early youth he showed a driving will and a passionate desire to modernize his tradition-bound country and to free it from fear of its neighbors.

Gigantic too was his native Russia. The land area of the Russia of Peter's time was nearly twice the size of today's United States of America. Long before Peter was born, the Russians as a separate people were extending their boundaries to include a wide variety of non-Russian peoples. The city of Moscow became the center of an Orthodox Christian state that gathered in other cities and territories. In the 1500s the ruler called Ivan the Terrible adopted the title *czar* (from the Latin *Caesar*). He broke the hold of the aristocratic class and kept expanding Russia by military conquest. Over the next hundred years Russia

109

pushed eastward into Siberia, the northern part of Asia. At its peak under the czars, the Russian empire would cover one sixth of the land surface of the globe.

So Peter did not begin the expansion process. He carried on, by his own unique methods, the aims of the Romanov dynasty. His father, Alexis, had tried to modernize the army and was the first czar to think of modernizing agriculture and industry as well. But his way of doing things would not be Peter's way.

Peter was born in 1672, the son of Alexis and his second wife, Natalia. Four years later Alexis died, and there was a vicious struggle for the throne. It ended with young Peter sharing power with a half brother, Ivan, both under the control of an older half sister, Sophia, as the regent. Finally, after the death of Ivan in 1696, Peter became sole ruler at the age of twenty-four.

How well was he prepared to rule? Warfare was taken as the prime occupation for any czar. In the nursery Peter played with toy soldiers, drums, cannons, and bows and arrows. A tutor inspired him with glowing stories of the military deeds of earlier czars. The boy knew that his father had led troops in battle. As Peter grew older, to toy weapons were added a grown-up's spades, hammers, and mason's tools.

When still a boy, Peter formed military squads of servants and young noblemen. But Peter's strongest love was for the sea, although Russia was a landlocked country and he would not see the ocean until he was twenty-one. The youngster played with toy boats and delighted in collecting maritime charts and ships' engravings. The most fun came from sailing an old English dinghy he found on a country estate.

As for more formal education, there was very little of it. He had no basic schooling in the fundamentals. Peter's handwriting and spelling were faulty early on and never improved. He did not benefit from a university education because there were no universities in the Russia of his time, nor even any public schools. For the most part only clerks and churchmen were literate.

What did help Peter's training was the presence of foreign specialists in Moscow. They had been arriving in Russia for more than a hundred years now, so many of them that Czar Alexis had given these military, diplomatic, and commercial people a separate neighborhood called the Foreign Quarter.

The foreigners were not warmly welcomed, either by the upper class or the peasantry. They were suspected of being dangerous heretics, at best only a necessary evil. Their Western ways of thinking and dressing and behaving did not reach beyond their own circle. Publishing and printing were controlled by the Church; few secular works ever reached print. And there were no Russian newspapers or journals; no plays, no poetry, no philosophy were published.

Young Peter could often be found in the Foreign Quarter. He made several friends there who helped shape his thinking. He often visited their homes and attended their banquets and weddings. From Scots and Swiss veterans who were now officers in the Russian army, Peter learned about the art of war as well as about life in the West. Whether they were Catholic or Protestant, the foreigners tended to be flexible in their thinking, and they moved Peter toward religious tolerance. To the young czar they appeared more cultivated, more knowledgeable about scientific and industrial matters than his own people. From them he picked up a working knowledge of some foreign languages. If he visited their homes and attended their weddings, he may have been influenced by women too.

Peter was learning how wide the gap was between Russia and the major western European countries. All of them had universities, schools, academies of science, theaters, libraries, newspapers. True, the common people everywhere remained illiterate. But in Old Russia ignorance of anything but religious duty was cultivated. Peter soon realized that a good education was the key to unlocking Russian potential. "I am a student and I seek teachers," he once said. Those words would symbolize state policy during his reign.

In 1689 Peter married Evdokia Lopukhina, a noblewoman. He was seventeen and she, twenty. It was a marriage arranged by Peter's mother to tell the world that her son was now a man. It became clear that Peter had little time for a bride who, people said, was pretty, yes, but dull, and no match for him. Nevertheless they had two children: Alexis, his heir, and then another boy who died in infancy.

The young couple began to quarrel bitterly when Evdokia learned that

Peter was having affairs with other women. They were divorced after ten stormy years. Later he would marry one of his lovers, a peasant girl who had served in his household and whom he made his empress, Catherine I.

His second wife was a match for Peter. She was good-looking, strong, shared his sense of humor, and could even joke about the extramarital affairs he continued to have—a tolerance many queens of that day showed for their husbands. Catherine bore several children, but only two—Anna and Elizabeth—survived beyond childhood.

What did Peter look like? The Frenchman Saint-Simon, who knew the czar, described him in his memoirs:

> The czar was a very tall man, exceedingly well-made, rather thin, his face somewhat round, a high forehead, good eyebrows, a rather short nose, but not too short, and large at the end, rather thick lips, complexion reddish brown, good black eyes, large, bright, piercing, and well open; his look majestic and gracious when he liked, but when otherwise, severe and stern with a twitching of the face, not often occurring, but which appeared to contract his eyes, and all his physiognomy, and was frightful to see; it lasted for a moment, gave him a wild and terrible air, and passed away.

When Peter's mother died in 1694 he became more active in government. He wanted to strengthen Russia's position among the other powers and made military or diplomatic moves to that end wherever he saw openings. He warred twice against Turkey to capture Azov, a Turkish coastal fort. He succeeded on his second try, but only after the first defeat led him to create the naval fleet that Russia had lacked. He had shipyards built hastily, and he himself worked alongside the thousands of conscripted laborers and foreign craftsmen. They produced the river craft and seagoing vessels needed to support an army of seventy thousand troops and to blockade the port to prevent Turkish reinforcements. The speed of this massive effort, the muster of manpower, and the iron command from above became typical of Peter's career. By now he was the sole ruler, for his co-czar, Ivan, had died in 1696.

His success at Azov led Peter to attempt more ambitious policies. He hoped to cement alliances with other nations against common enemies while learning all he could about their expertise and technology. In 1697 he sent abroad an embassy of fifty-five nobles and two hundred attendants nominally headed by an army officer. But Peter himself was among them, traveling incognito under the name of Peter Mikhailov. The disguise was almost a joke, for the towering czar was recognized everywhere he went.

A German princess who dined and danced with Peter wrote that "The Czar is very tall, his features are fine, and his figure very noble. He has great vivacity of mind. . . . It could be wished that his manners were a little less rustic. He told us that he worked in building ships, showed us his hands, and made us touch the callous places that had been caused by work. He has a very good heart. . . . He did not get drunk in our presence but we had hardly left when the people of his suite made ample amends."

When they reached the Netherlands, Peter headed for Zaandam, a shipbuilding center. There he stayed in a workman's cottage while he spent a week laboring alongside the shipwrights, trying to master their craft. Then on to Amsterdam to study the shipyards, workshops, and factories. He came away with a knowledge of clock making, copper engraving, and even dentistry. (At home again he would delight in performing dentistry on friends unlucky enough to complain of toothache in front of him.) He watched autopsies performed so he could better understand human anatomy.

He visited Dutch homes to see how families lived, shopped in their markets, and learned to mend his own clothes and repair his own shoes. He sat elbow to elbow in their saloons to drink beer and wine with the Dutch. Given access to their best specialists, he studied military engineering, microscopy, architecture, and mechanics. What other royal figure ever tried to soak up so much life and learning?

After spending four months in the Netherlands as "carpenter Peter of Zaandam," he crossed the English Channel to continue his studies in England for another few months. He visited the arsenal, the Royal Observatory, and the

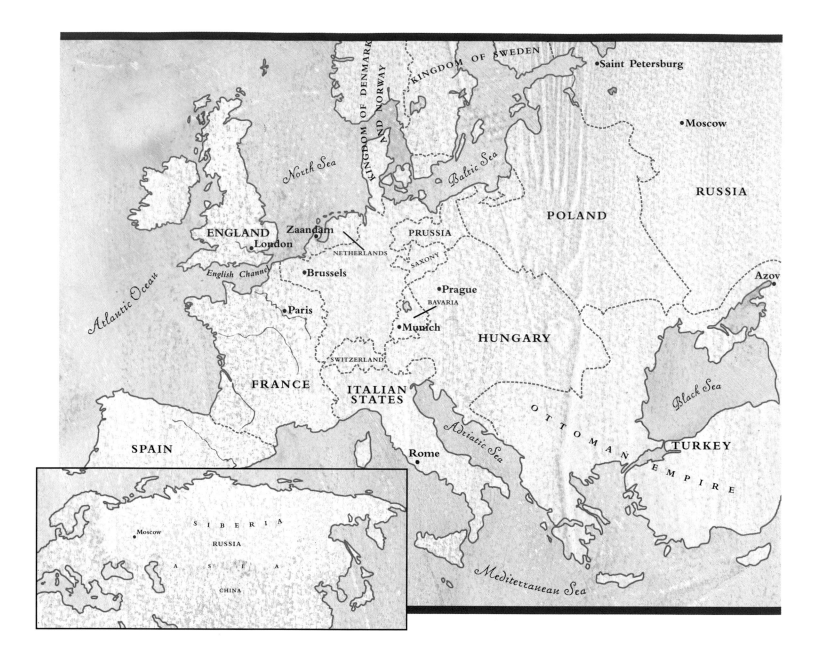

Royal Society; went to Anglican services and Quaker meetings; saw Oxford University; and dropped in on the theater and on Parliament.

For a while Peter and some of his group stayed in a house loaned him by the diarist John Evelyn. That poor man found that they had been "right nasty," breaking three hundred glass panes, destroying twenty-one pictures, causing an explosion on the kitchen floor, and wrecking a holly hedge. It only confirmed the common prejudice against those "barbarous" Russians.

While a failure in making any diplomatic gains, the embassy did produce some practical results. Peter learned a lot, impressed royalty, and hired more than five hundred military and technical experts to teach their skills to Russians. He brought home two hundred and sixty chests packed with weapons, tools, sailcloth, cork, anchors, scientific instruments—and a stuffed crocodile.

Gone eighteen months, Peter returned home in September 1698 ready to launch a program of westernization. He came ahead of schedule, for word had reached him of a revolt of the *streltsy*. These were nonnoble regiments of servicemen who did escort and guard duty during peacetime and fought in wartime. When not on duty they carried on small businesses and trade. Their revolt was prompted by the fear that Peter, who wanted to westernize the military, might abolish their corps. But by the time Peter reached Moscow, government troops had crushed the revolt. After a long investigation and trial of the rebels that included torture, 1,182 were executed (five by Peter's own hand), and 601 flogged and banished. Peter's punishments were a warning to others. They showed how ruthless he could be in getting rid of opposition.

"Now I need a new army," Peter said. No more reliance on the old mixture of *streltsy*, foreign mercenaries, and peasants "volunteered" by their landlords. He built a standing army of 210,000 men by drafting one man from every twenty peasant households. He dressed his troops in Western-style uniforms and drilled them in Western tactics. Their term of service, in every rank, was for life. Shipbuilding too raced ahead, and soon the Russian navy had forty-eight ships of the line, eight hundred smaller ships, and twenty-eight thousand sailors.

The first target of Peter's new military was Sweden. At that time Sweden included both Finland and part of what is now western Russia. He thought that neighbor, headed by eighteen-year-old Charles XII, would be an easy victim. But the war went badly. The Swedish king was a bold and gifted leader, and his much smaller force almost wiped out the Russians. From that bitter outcome Peter learned that victory would require more time and greater effort. He improved the military's equipment and training, copied the English flintlock musket, opened an artillery school, and was soon producing more cannon than

Sweden. By 1704 the Russians were able to do much better against the Swedes, captured the Neva delta, massacred the area's Swedish inhabitants, and won access to the Gulf of Finland, a long-desired outlet to the Baltic Sea.

With the Neva delta under his control, Peter could launch the development of a new seaport city—Saint Petersburg. But as great a project as this was, it was only one element of his program to reform Russia and the Russians. The day after his return from abroad he had shaved off his beard, and ordered all other men to do the same. Only mustaches could remain. Beards were almost a religious symbol in Russia; to be without one was believed heretical. But Peter commanded: do it or pay a stiff fine. Beardlessness was a sign of being a modern man. To be truly civilized, Peter said, Russians must stop being childish, selfish, violent in their behavior.

His next reform was to get rid of Russia's traditional costume. Both men and women were ordered to adopt Western dress. He ended the seclusion of women, urging them to drop their traditional veils, to enter social gatherings, to learn to dance, to seek education, and to collect Western books and even to read them. He forbade parents forcing their children to marry against their will.

The greatest barrier to change was the Church. The clergy knew that Peter's reforms would reduce their prestige and power. Peter set out to limit the large numbers who entered the many monasteries, and to divert to his own treasury the great revenues of those institutions. When the Orthodox patriarch died in 1700, Peter did not appoint a successor. Instead, like Henry VIII of England, he made himself head of the Church. Later he abolished the office of patriarch and appointed in its place a group of clergy subject to the government.

Most of the clergy gave in to him. The few who resisted were arrested, banished to Siberia, imprisoned for life, and some were even tortured or burned to death. In general, said one historian, Peter's religious reforms were his most lasting. "They ended the Middle Ages in Russia."

From domination by priests and landlords, Peter's Russia moved to regimentation by the state. The nobles were subjected to the will of the czar. He made them serve the state and ranked them by the importance of the social services they performed. Under his dominance the nobles felt humiliated; to be in "the ruling class" now meant little or nothing. A new merit class arose, made up of officials in the military and the bureaucracy. The czar appointed members of a senate who managed the bureaus that handled the diverse interests of government, such as taxes, commerce, foreign affairs, the military, and the law.

The people of each city were divided into classes: merchants and the professions at the top, then the craftsmen, and at the bottom the wage earners. Only the first class could be elected to municipal councils and only the first two classes could vote. But all male taxpayers could take part in town meetings.

While Peter encouraged industry, he did almost nothing for agriculture. He failed to eliminate serfdom; instead, he extended it to industry. To staff the expanding factories he forced peasants to become industrial workers. Industrialists bought serfs from landlords and set them to work in factories.

Peter was convinced that reform could not be won without compulsion, "for our people are like children," he said, "who never want to begin the alphabet unless they are compelled by their teachers. It seems very hard to them at first, but when they have learnt it they are thankful."

Factories turning out products had to have some means to market them. Peter encouraged commerce by raising the social status of merchants. He built canals to connect rivers so that trade could move along water, for Russian distances were vast, and the few roads that existed were in terrible shape.

Peter needed huge sums to pay for his wars and other enterprises. Heavy taxation was the obvious way to raise capital. But he was always short of money because there was widespread corruption and dishonesty, despite brutal punishments and the death penalty for such crimes.

Yes, it was hard to transform people, harder than to reform the military, the administration, the Church. When Peter decided to create a new capital for Russia, it meant expanding his royal powers even more. By abandoning Moscow, the ancient capital, in favor of inventing Saint Petersburg, he was rejecting Russia's past.

The city was begun in 1703, planted on territory captured from the Swedes. It was not an ideal place, for much of the site was marshland that often flooded. The foundations had to be laid on piles. The vast construction enter-

Who were the Russians?

There are no exact figures, but estimates for the early 1700s give a total population of sixteen million. Of these, thirteen million were peasants, six hundred thousand were townspeople, and one million three hundred thousand were landowners, clergy, and military. All Russian peasants were serfs, bound to the service of either individuals or institutions. Serfs could move only with someone's approval—nobles, churches, monasteries, the state. In a sense all peasants were bound to the czar, regardless of provisional owner, because the monarch had first call on their revenues and labor. "The peasants are perfect slaves," wrote a foreign observer. "They can call nothing their own."

Peter often spoke of running his government "for the common good." That was only an abstraction, for he couldn't care less about the suffering of the masses. Serfdom to him was just one more way of satisfying the state's demands.

Still, peasants were people. They felt, they dreamed, they desired, they hoped. They were not always mute or passive. They had grievances and the courage at times to rebel against oppression and poverty. Their most common protest took the form of flight; they ran away.

It was hard to tell the difference between peasants and workers in Peter's time. The czar's increasing demand for labor in shipbuilding, transport, mining, construction, and the military created a bottomless pit in which countless peasants perished.

prise consumed the blood and bone of tens of thousands of conscripted laborers. They were paid half a ruble per month, a starvation wage that they supplemented by begging and stealing. Thousands of prisoners of war, peasants, and criminals died on the job from overwork, malnutrition, and disease.

Peter moved his family to the new city in 1710 and declared it the capital of Russia in 1712. When he died in 1725, St. Petersburg's population was forty thousand, and the city was far from complete. It grew over time into one of Europe's most magnificent cities. It became a major port, a commercial and industrial center, a brilliant cultural community, and a huge military garrison. Today it contains about 4.5 million citizens. One of the city's great landmarks is the Bronze Horseman, a statue of Peter the Great presented to the city by the empress Catherine the Great.

When the Russian Revolution occurred in 1917, Moscow became the capital again, and St. Petersburg was renamed Leningrad, in honor of the Communist leader Lenin. But in 1991, as the Soviet system collapsed, the citizens voted to restore the name St. Petersburg.

While pouring energy into changing the economic and political life of the country, Peter did not neglect Russian culture. He felt it was ridden with superstition, which he hoped to replace with education and science. He reformed both the calendar and the alphabet, launched the first Russian newspaper, and published books on science and technology. He built technical institutes and ordered the sons of the nobility to attend them. In each province he set up schools, but few survived. He opened a theater in Moscow and brought in European actors to perform comedies and tragedies. Western musicians too arrived to form orchestras. Peter bought paintings and statues, mostly Italian, for an art museum in St. Petersburg and opened it to all, free of charge. Foreign architects were commissioned to design palaces and churches.

But when, in 1724, a courageous Russian published a book that denounced the oppression of the peasantry and called for an impartial court system to administer justice fairly, he was thrown into prison, where he died. In the West, the creators of culture looked for royal and aristocratic patronage, but they were not wholly dependent on it. In Peter's Russia cultural affairs were in the state's control. An artist could go only so far without risking disapproval, or even death.

Resentment of Peter's reforms grew year by year. It was not that the Russians were unused to poverty and despotism. But many felt Peter's reign had

palace of St. Petersburg

become unbearable—heavier taxes, forced labor, mass deaths in warfare, and interminable exhaustion from all the burdens heaped upon them. Beggary and crime increased; the nobles hated being forced to serve the state and resented the rise of the business class. The peasants and the clergy also had strong reason to hate what was demanded of them. How could anyone love a monarch so ready to unleash violence against anyone who differed with him?

Even Peter's son Alexis, whom the czar planned would inherit the realm and carry on his reforms, had come to dislike the changes his father introduced and the methods used to enforce them. Totally unlike his father, the son was small, timid, and weak, with no taste for the military life. He married a princess, lost her a year later in childbirth, and drank heavily. When Peter accused him of plotting with others against him, Alexis confessed—under torture—and in 1718 died in prison.

Despite his giant physique, Peter was exhausted by decades of wars, revolts, violence, and unending labors. Disease weakened him, and crude medical treatment only worsened his condition. He died in 1725. He was fifty-two years old.

When Peter died, he left an exhausted Russia. During his reign the country's population dropped 20 percent. Then came a series of short-reigned rulers. The strong regular army Peter had built was neglected. No one took the throne who would use this powerful instrument until the reign of Catherine II (Catherine the Great) in the second half of the eighteenth century.

"Of all imperial Russia's rulers" wrote the historian J. M. Roberts, "the one who made the most memorable use of the autocracy and most deeply shaped its character was Peter the Great. . . . When he died something had been done to Russia which could never be quite eradicated." Yes, agrees a modern Russian historian, E. V. Anisimov: "The era of the Petrine reforms was the time of the foundation of the totalitarian state, the graphic preaching and inculcation into mass consciousness of the strong personality—the boss, the 'father of the nation,' the 'teacher of the people.'" Among Russian citizens today some nominate Peter the Great as their "most admired ruler" while others regard him as "the devil incarnate."

Peter was off the stage of history as the first quarter of the eighteenth century ended. In the last quarter of that century the Enlightenment ideals of self-government and individual freedom led to the founding of the democratic American republic and to a revolution in France that overthrew the monarchy. Could the czar have imagined such immense change happening so quickly?

A Note on Sources

Biographical research always presents problems, for no part of the world's past is without confusion and complexity. I have tried, within the limited space of these essays, to make each king's reign understandable by using all the sources available to me. But when you delve back into the lives of people who lived thousands or even a few hundred years ago, you run into difficulties. The further back in time you go, the scarcer are the sources. Sometimes little or nothing exists in writing. That turns the biographer to nonliterary sources: coins, inscriptions, shrines, monuments, stelae, reliefs. What the archaeologists unearth, though fragmentary, is invaluable.

Even when you have what seems to be ample evidence—documents, letters, memoirs, diaries, autobiographies—you need to be wary, for this material is always shaped by people with their own motives. No one can be purely objective. People wish to make themselves or others look good—or bad. Then there is the fact that, until fairly recently, most history was written by the elite, the dominant members of society. How the men and women in the lower ranks thought and felt was rarely recorded in history except in the context of violent acts of resistance and rebellion.

Out of what the sources contain, the biographer seeks to create some arrangement or pattern in the life he or she has studied. Documentary evidence can be used in imaginative ways without departing from the truth. You try to give a form to flux, to impose a design upon chronology. My task has included finding a way to re-create the world of each king's life span as the king experienced it.

Bibliography

The sources used for each king's story are arranged here by chapter. For more general information on historical periods, from various perspectives, I referred to many other works. Among these were:

Braudel, Fernand. *A History of Civilization.* New York: Penguin, 1993.

———. *The Wheels of Commerce: Civilization and Capitalism, Fifteenth to Eighteenth Century.* New York: Harper, 1982.

Commire, Anne, ed. *Historical World Leaders.* 4 vols. Detroit: Gale, 1994.

Davies, Norman. *Europe: A History.* New York: Oxford University Press, 1996.

Diamond, Jared. *Guns, Germs and Steel.* New York: Norton, 1997.

Dupuy, R. Ernest, and Trevor N. Dupuy. *The Harper Encyclopedia of Military History.* New York: HarperCollins, 1993.

East, W. Gordon. *The Geography Behind History.* New York: Norton, 1967.

Hale, John. *The Civilization of Europe in the Renaissance.* New York: Touchstone, 1993.

Keegan, John. *A History of Warfare.* New York: Knopf, 1993.

Knapton, Ernest John. *Europe: 1415–1815.* New York: Scribner's, 1958.

Landes, David S. *The Wealth and Poverty of Nations.* New York: Norton, 1998.

McNeill, William. *The Rise of the West: A History of the Human Community.* Chicago: University of Chicago Press, 1963.

Parry, J. H. *The Age of Reconnaissance.* Berkeley: University of California Press, 1981.

Reynolds, Robert. *Europe Emerges: 600–1750.* Madison: University of Wisconsin Press, 1967.

Roberts, J. M. *Penguin History of the World.* New York: Penguin, 1990.

Tuchman, Barbara. *The March of Folly.* New York: Ballantine, 1985.

HAMMURABI

Kramer, Samuel Noah. *Cradle of Civilization.* New York: Time-Life, 1967.

Mackenzie, Donald A. *Mythology of the Babylonian People.* London: Buchan, 1915.

DAVID

Alter, Robert. *The David Story.* New York: Norton, 1999.

Cahill, Thomas. *The Gifts of the Jews.* New York: Doubleday, 1998.

Deen, Edith. *All the Women of the Bible.* New York: Harper, 1990.

Fox, Everett, ed. *Give Us a King! Samuel, Saul, and David.* New York: Ktaav, 1989.

Keller, Werner. *The Bible as History.* New York: Barnes & Noble, 1995.

Schwarz, Leo W., ed. *Great Ages and Ideas of the Jewish People.* New York: Random House, 1956.

Telushkin, Joseph. *Jewish Literacy.* New York: Morrow, 1991.

ALEXANDER THE GREAT

Briant, Pierre. *Alexander the Great: Man of Action, Man of Spirit.* New York: Abrams, 1996.

Burn, A. R. *The Penguin History of Greece.* New York: Penguin, 1990.

Fuller, J. F. C. *The Generalship of Alexander the Great.* New York: Wordsworth, 1980.

Green, Peter. *Alexander to Actium: The Historical Evolution of the Hellenistic Age.* Berkeley: University of California Press, 1990.

Hammond, A. G. L. *The Genius of Alexander the Great* Chapel Hill: University of North Carolina Press, 1997.

Kitto, H. D. F. *The Greeks.* New York: Penguin, 1991.

O'Brien, John Maxwell. *Alexander the Great—The Invisible Enemy: A Biography.* New York: Routledge, 1992.

Pomeroy, Sara B., ed. *Ancient Greece: A Political, Social and Cultural History.* New York: Oxford University Press, 1999.

ATTILA

Haworth, Patrick. *Attila: King of the Huns.* Carlisle, Pa.: John Kellman, 1994.

McCullough, David W. *Chronicle of the Barbarians.* New York: Times Books, 1998.

CHARLEMAGNE

Cantor, Norman E. *The Civilization of the Middle Ages.* New York: HarperCollins, 1993.

Collins, Roger. *Charlemagne.* Toronto: University of Toronto Press, 1998.

Lopez, Robert S. *The Birth of Europe.* New York: Evans, 1967.

Riche, Pierre. *Daily Life in the World of Charlemagne.* Philadelphia: University of Pennsylvania Press, 1988.

KUBLAI KHAN

Cotterell, Arthur. *East Asia.* London: John Murray, 1993.

Paludan, Ann. *Chronicles of the Chinese Emperors.* New York: Thames and Hudson, 1998.

Rossabi, Morris. *Khubilai Khan: His Life and Times.* Berkeley: University of California Press, 1988.

MANSA MUSA

Burns, Kephra. *Mansa Musa: The Lion of Mali.* New York: Harcourt Brace, 2000.

Davidson, Basil. *African Civilization Revisited: From Antiquity to Modern Times.* Trenton, N.J.: Africa World Press, 1991.

————. *The African Slave Trade.* Boston: Little Brown, 1980.

Gates, Henry Louis, Jr. *Wonders of the African World.* New York: Knopf, 1999.

Gordon, Murray. *Slavery in the Arab World.* New York: New Amsterdam Books, 1992.

Thobhani, Akbaroli. *Mansa Musa: The Golden Age of Ancient Mali.* Dubuque, Iowa: Kendall/Hunt, 1998.

ATAHUALPA

Editors of Time-Life Books. *Incas: Lords of Gold and Glory.* Alexandria, Va.: Time-Life, 1992.

Hyams, Edwin, and George Ordish. *The Last of the Incas: The Rise and Fall of an American Empire.* New York: Barnes & Noble, 1996.

Moseley, Michael E. *The Incas and Their Ancestors.* New York: Thames and Hudson, 1993.

Wright, Louis B. *Gold, Glory and the Gospel.* New York: Atheneum, 1970.

LOUIS XIV

Braudel, Fernand. *The Identity of France.* New York: Harper, 1988.

Durant, Will, and Ariel Durant. *The Age of Louis XIV.* New York: MJF Books, 1963.

Goubert, Pierre. *Louis XIV and Twenty Million Frenchmen.* New York: Vintage, 1972.

Mitford, Nancy. *The Sun King.* New York: Penguin, 1966.

PETER THE GREAT

Hughes, Lindsey. *Russia in the Age of Peter the Great.* New Haven: Yale University Press, 1998.

Massie, Robert K. *Peter the Great: His Life and World.* New York: Ballantine, 1981.

Warnes, David. *Chronicles of the Russian Tsars.* New York: Thames and Hudson, 1999.

Index